JUICY GOSSIP

candy apple books...
just for you.
sweet. fresh. fun.
take a bite!

JUICY GOSSIP

by Erin Downing

SCHOLASTIC INC.

New York Toronto London Auckland Sydney
Mexico City New Delhi Hong Kong Buenos Aires

ISBN-13: 978-0-545-10066-3
ISBN-10: 0-545-10066-6

12 11 10 9 8 7 6 5 4 3 2 1   9 10 11 12 13 14/0

Printed in the U.S.A.   40
First printing, June 2009

For Robin Wasserman
Who gave me the courage and confidence to go for it . . . and
who always keeps my gossip a secret.

Special thanks to Zack and Alex Przybylski — my cool
cousins. Also thanks to Shannon Penney, who has been a
treat to work with.

CHAPTER ONE

I wish I could go to boarding school.

French boarding school.

J'adore croissants. And cutie-pie French boys. They sound so romantic when they talk. (Boys, not croissants.) Especially when they say things like "*j'adore croissants.*"

Of course, I've never actually met a French guy (nor have I heard one say "*j'adore croissants,*" but that's completely beside the point). So maybe I'm just thinking about Michael Hollings, who is my partner in French class and has his French accent down to an art. "*J'adore . . .*" It rolls off his tongue like a buttery, jammy croissant. "*J'adore . . .*"

"*Oui,* Jenna?" Madame Fishman, my French teacher, is staring at me. It's the middle of third period and I'm not paying attention.

I have other things to think about.

I clear my throat, which sounds similar to my French pronunciation. Unlike Michael Hollings, I do *not* have my French accent down to an art. "*Oui*, madame?"

Michael Hollings, sitting next to me, looks at me like I'm crazy. I think maybe I'd been muttering "*j'adore*" under my breath.

"Do you have something to say to the class?" Madame Fishman's eyes look like bulgy fish eyeballs, which always cracks me up. I wonder if that's why she married Mr. Fishman. She must have known it was a super-hilarious coincidence that a fish-eyed lady would marry into a name like Fishman.

But this is so not the point.

I can't help but widen my eyes back at her when I say, "*Non*, madame. I'm just practicing. *Practiquant*!"

Madame Fishman looks delighted that I have mastered such an important French verb, and moves on.

I have become an expert at not paying attention in French class. I prefer to spend most of class admiring Michael Hollings. Unfortunately, my crush doesn't go both ways. I'm pretty sure Michael doesn't even know my last name. I think

Michael might also be kind of rude — or maybe he just doesn't like to talk. But his absolute cuteness makes up for it.

Almost.

Now he turns toward me and shakes his head, giving me this look like, *Why are you talking to yourself, you nut? What is wrong with you?* (He doesn't say that or anything, but his expression makes me pretty certain that's what he's thinking.)

Nice, I think, my face reddening. *That's nice, Michael.* There's nothing truly wrong with me, but there are definitely some things that are making me the teensiest bit distracted. I sort of wish I could tell Michael just how much is wrong with my life right now. Then he would understand why I'm muttering strange French phrases under my breath. Because my life is about to get pretty bad . . . and *that* is why I want to go to boarding school.

I've decided to move to France because my parents, Stew and Liz Sampson, are opening a fruit juice bar in the food court at the mall. The little space between Sbarro Pizza and the Wok 'N' Walk will soon be home to Juice It, the latest in a long line of Stew and Liz's embarrassing professional undertakings.

My best friend Keisha Morris's parents both work at an ad agency. My neighbor, Cassidy Conlan, is the publisher of *Splash!*, a home design magazine. Mrs. Jackson, who comes over for coffee with my mom, is a civics teacher, for crying out loud. These are all normal careers.

My parents' new venture? Not so much.

Some people may think this whole juice-bar-at-the-mall thing would be kind of fun. Or cool, even. Not me. Not only do I despise the mall (more on that later), but I also have a strong dislike of fruit. That makes a fruit juice bar *at* the mall incredibly unpleasant for me — especially since I have to work there.

I'm sure you're wondering: "Who dislikes fruit? That's just weird." Well, I consider that one of my quirks, and I have very normal reasons for it.

First off, kiwi fruit has fur and papaya smells like armpits — enough said. Berries have tiny little seeds that shimmy between my teeth and force me to floss. Citrus fruit tastes like cleaning fluid. And I once ate so much pineapple during a family trip to Florida that all my taste buds got sizzled off. Seriously. Sizzled off. I couldn't taste anything for a week.

So fruit juice + me do not = ♥. And the mall? Like I said, we'll get to that. But for now, just know that I'm not psyched about my parents' decision.

I personally find this career venture more than a little embarrassing. It feels too much like the time my dad started to sell those weird vegetable storage bags online, or when my stepmom, Liz, opened a store downtown that sold only beads and ballet shoes. Go figure. Now it's a juice bar at the mall. Totally random, and totally yuck.

I exhale a huge sigh, and Michael pulls his book farther away on our shared desk. I can't tell if Michael really *is* trying to get away from me because he thinks I'm a total weirdo, or if I'm imagining the whole thing. To be honest, Michael is sort of a mystery to me. A quiet, brooding, mystery boy . . . *ooh la la*, like a French poet or film star or something!

Michael is also totally out of my league. He's always hanging out with Robbie Prinzo and Jeremy Rosenberg, and he has a million girls oohing over him all the time. I wonder if he ever talks to any of them. Well, he doesn't talk to *me* — in English, anyway — and that's what matters.

Just then, the bell rings, marking the end of class. I grab my workbook and head into the hall. I have early lunch, so I rummage around for my peanut butter and honey bagel sandwich in the mess of sticky notes that fills my locker, and walk down the main hall toward the journalism room.

Almost every day, I spend both my lunch period and fourth period in Mrs. Jensen's English classroom, which I've dubbed "the journalism room." I have journalism class fourth period, so I usually just bring my lunch and go to class really early. I mean, I could either spend my lunch period in the cafeteria text messaging with people like Stacey Smith and her BFF of the week, or spend that time productively working on the school paper.

I'm not naive enough to think that Stacey Smith would ever text message me. For one thing, I don't have a cell phone. My parents think cell phones give you brain tumors, so they won't buy a family plan. But my lack of phone is totally not the point, since Stacey Smith probably doesn't even know who I am.

Stacey and I are in the same homeroom and her locker is near mine, but I don't think she's ever even glanced at me. There are four different elementary schools that feed into Washington Middle School, and four hundred of us get smushed together in each grade. I'm not a total outcast, but I'm definitely not one of Washington's Seventh Grade Snobs (my term, not theirs). I'm just Jenna — not popular, not unpopular. Just . . . there.

The Snobs rule Washington, and people like me — Jenna Sampson, editor of the school newspaper — are pretty much invisible. It doesn't really bother me most of the time. I would much rather be known for my probing journalistic skills than the color of my barrettes. (Are barrettes even in style? You get my point.)

But I always seem to be the last to know everything that's going on, which isn't really the best way to succeed as a journalist. Aren't journalists supposed to be in the know? I have no clue if Heidi from *The Hills* is a good guy or a bad guy. I couldn't tell you if black is fashionable this year. And don't even get me started on who's dating who in Hollywood — or who's dating who in the seventh grade at my school. I just can't keep up with it all.

Sometimes, I think it would be nice to be a teensy-eensy bit more popular. Not just so I don't feel like I'm totally out of it, but also so that certain people (ahem, Michael Hollings) would know I exist outside of French class. That wouldn't be *so* bad.

"Hey! Jenna!" I turn and spot my best friend Keisha's thick black curls bouncing down the hallway. She's waving, as though I wouldn't see her otherwise. But since she's, like, a foot taller than anyone else at school, she's pretty hard to miss. "Cafeteria today?" she asks, walking up next to me.

"I have six articles to write before we go to print next week," I say, blatantly using the paper as an excuse not to go to the cafeteria. The cafeteria gives me the creeps. It smells like feet from the back-to-school dance a few weeks ago (you have to take off your shoes during dances for some reason, and Jeremy Rosenberg's feet are *stinky*), and Keisha and I can never find a table that hasn't been claimed by some clique or another. "I need to get to work. There's a school board referendum they're trying to pass next month, and it's majorly important."

Keisha rolls her eyes. "Ick, Jenna. That sounds so boring."

"It's important," I protest as we pass the center stairs. "The school board's decisions affect us!" I fully realize how lame this sounds. But as a true journalist, I know this stuff is important to follow . . . even if it is a little bland. "We still have some space to fill in next week's paper, if you want to write a few more articles."

"Groan," Keisha replies as we walk down the

hall toward Mrs. J's room. "I wrote two articles for your paper last week. That's my monthly limit."

"Keish," I say, looking at her sternly. "Don't call it *my* paper. It's the *school's* paper."

Keisha looks right back at me. Her stares are fierce. "Jenna, you care about the paper more than anyone else. The paper lives and breathes with you and only you."

"That's not true!" I push the door to the journalism room open. Keisha follows me inside the empty classroom.

"But you're the editor," Keisha declares. "Mrs. Jensen chose you over Chris Dotman because you really, truly care about the newspaper."

"I care, but that doesn't mean people read it," I grumble. "I need to work really hard as editor this year to prove that a seventh grader can make people want to read the *Washington News*."

I was just named editor last week, partly because only one other guy really wanted the job — and he didn't even submit his application essay in time. Suffice it to say, the newspaper isn't exactly popular. But my dream is that I can get people to actually read it by making a great paper that everyone will love.

You have to apply to be on the newspaper staff at the end of sixth or seventh grade. Anyone at school can write articles for the paper, but you can only get credit for taking the journalism class one year. Usually the class doesn't even fill up.

There are sixteen of us on staff who are responsible for editing and designing the paper each week, but we use other students (like Keisha) to write most of the articles — when we can find kids who are willing. I was just a writer for the paper last year, but this year I'm on staff — and the editor.

"Jenna, you were the best choice — you were a shoo-in for editor. Hey, are you coming to our game tomorrow?" Keisha politely changes the subject, settling into one of the desks at the back of the classroom. She's fully aware that I'm super-defensive of the paper and hate that hardly anyone reads it — so I don't really like to talk about it.

"Argh." I cringe. "I have to go to the mall tomorrow afternoon to help my parents get the store ready for the opening on Saturday." I don't need to tell Keisha what "the store" is. She's even more horrified than I am about my parents' embarrassing new juice bar. Best friends are good like that.

"But I'm a starter!" Keisha is a midfielder on Washington's soccer team. She sat on the bench most of last season, but she practiced super-hard all summer and now she's really good. Stacey Smith is the star of the team, but I'm pretty sure Keisha is the better player now — even better than all the eighth graders. Keisha would never say that, but I know it's true. "Jenna, I need you to be there. You're my good-luck charm."

I grin, flattered. "I can send a melon in my place. You can just call me Fruity McFruiterson for the next few years, until my parents realize that a food court juice bar is a bad idea." The image of a melon sitting in the stands at the WMS soccer field makes me giggle.

Keisha cracks up, too. "The worst part about this whole food court juice bar thing is that you don't even *like* the mall. I mean, if you were Stacey Smith or Jasmine Chen or someone, it wouldn't be so awful. At least you could go shopping for a new look on your breaks."

The thing is: I'm not a shopper. I'm not a fashionista. In fact, I can't even match black and pink together correctly. I *despise* shopping. Keisha knows this as well as anyone. I usually just sort of get dressed. End of story.

My best friend sizes me up now, as though it's the first time she's seen me all day. She looks concerned. "Speaking of new looks . . ." That's the cool thing about Keisha — she just speaks her mind. I guess you could call her a loudmouth, but I've never cared. "What are you wearing today?"

For the record, I missed the lesson in what colors go together. My stepmom, Liz, wears only shades of khaki and chocolate, so I'm just lucky I didn't follow in those footsteps. "What do you mean?"

Keisha groans. "Your jeans have a hole in them. And is that your *brother's* sweater?"

I look down. Yup. "So?" I ask. "Writers never worry about fashion. We're supposed to look frazzled. I'm playing the part."

"You're playing it well."

"Keisha!" I grab a copy of the school newspaper from a full rack near Mrs. J's desk, and swat her with it. "That's not nice."

She shrugs. "Sorry. But it's true."

I guess I could be offended, but I'm used to the things Keisha says, and I'm comfortable with the way I dress. It's not terrible enough to get negative attention from the Seventh Grade Snobs, and it's not cool enough that anyone cares. It's fine, and that works for me.

Just then, Mrs. Jensen walks through the classroom door. She looks a little surprised to see us there, which is odd, since I spend almost every lunch period in her classroom. Mrs. J can be a little spacey sometimes, which is part of the reason I like her so much. "Hi, Mrs. J," I say, turning on the computer in the back corner of the room.

"Girls," she answers. Mrs. J isn't big on chatting, but today she looks like she has something more to say. "Jenna, we need to talk."

Yikes. She sounds a little like my dad does after I've forgotten to take the garbage out. That's his pet peeve — full garbage cans. Go figure. I can come up with a lot more important things to worry about in life. I sometimes tell him that when he scolds me for forgetting to empty the wastebasket in my room. He's not very fond of that, either. "What's wrong, Mrs. J?"

"Jenna, I was just in a meeting with Mrs. Liu." Mrs. Liu is our principal. She's really nice, but also sort of scary. She's very serious, and wears these abnormally high heels that clack angrily in the hallways. I'm pretty sure Mrs. Liu doesn't mean for her feet to sound angry, but they do.

Mrs. Jensen continues, "School funding is being cut, and Mrs. Liu and the rest of the Teachers' Committee are looking for ways to save some money."

"Okay . . ." I say. I'm not seeing what this has to do with me.

Mrs. Jensen sits on top of her desk. One of her legs dangles off the edge, and the way it swings back and forth is driving me crazy. Her toe taps nervously in midair.

"I'm sorry, Jenna," Mrs. Jensen says finally. "I know how much the newspaper means to you. But we have no choice — the newspaper is being cut."

CHAPTER TWO

I stand there, staring openmouthed at Mrs. J, who is still nervously wriggling her foot.

"Hold on," I say. "Did you say that the paper is being cut?" Keisha walks over to me and rests her hand on my back, well aware that I'm about to freak out. "Like, completely gone? No longer published?"

Mrs. Jensen nods, and I hang on to the edge of a desk for support. Without the newspaper to look forward to, the highlight of my day will be ... Michael Hollings? I don't think so. "What can I do to change this decision?" I'm trying to be mature, so I feel proud when this question comes out of my mouth.

"There isn't really anything you can do," Mrs. J says sadly. "The fact is, no one is reading the paper. Unless the whole school suddenly starts reading it, there just isn't a logical reason to keep printing it every week." She gestures to the full stack of unread, unclaimed newspapers next to her classroom door. "And I think that's unlikely to happen."

She has a point. No one reads the paper. "So what's going to happen to the journalism elective period?" I ask. There are sixteen of us and a handful of writers — like Keisha — who work on the paper. "Will we all have to switch to the fitness or theater or photography elective courses during fourth period?" Fitness? I shudder.

"Unfortunately, theater and photography are also in jeopardy — but the fitness program is safe, since it doesn't cost much money. Mrs. Liu and the Teachers' Committee are trying to save money by cutting the least popular programs first. Fourth period journalism will simply become a study hall."

Study hall? So I could be editor of . . . study hall? There has to be a better solution. "Mrs. J," I say, unrealistically hopeful all of a sudden. "What if people *did* start reading the paper? Could the Teachers' Committee's decision be reversed?"

Keisha is looking at me like I'm crazy. "Jenna," she blurts out, "that's *never* going to happen."

She slaps a hand over her mouth, clearly feeling a little bad about her comment. It's what we're all thinking, but she didn't have to say it.

Mrs. J looks at me and Keisha sort of pityingly. "Yes," she says, still tapping her foot up and down. "If you could boost readership, I think I could make a case for continuing to publish the newspaper. If not weekly, maybe monthly." She cringes. "But I'm talking about the whole student body . . . not just a few extra students picking up a copy now and then. You don't have a lot of time, Jenna — these changes will be happening next month."

"I hear you, Mrs. J." I sound very in control and confident, but inside I'm squirming. I don't know how, in a million years, I'm going to convince the rest of the sixth, seventh, and eighth grade classes that they should start reading the *Washington News*.

But it's pretty clear that I'm going to have to find a way.

After sixth period that day, we have assembly. The main purpose is to cheer for our football team's upcoming game against Penn, the other middle school in our town. They're also announcing the nominees for the Fall Carnival King and

Queen. The King and Queen are always eighth graders, but there are also a Prince and Princess from the seventh grade.

Keisha claims that it's a huge honor to be the Prince or Princess, but I wouldn't really know. That's just not my thing. We cover it in the paper, but I don't really care who gets nominated. I *do* like to go to Fall Carnival, which is always a total blast.

We have these "spirit assemblies" once a week. Our vice principal was a cheerleader in high school, and she's really into school spirit. She made weekly assemblies mandatory, which means every class gets shortened by five minutes on Thursdays. It's pretty nice.

The spirit assemblies have always been a great place for me to figure out what the rest of the school is all pumped up about, and what subjects we should be covering in the next week's newspaper. It's my chance to feel like I really know what's going on. But I guess I might not need to worry about that for much longer. Urgh.

As I walk into the gym, everyone's buzzing, happy for an excuse to be out of class. I look around for Keisha, but she's already sitting with a couple girls from her fifth period Spanish class, and that section of bleachers is full. Katy Gurtzke, one of the other seventh graders on the paper, is in the middle section alone, so I climb the steps and sit next to her.

"Hey," I say, plunking down on the bench. "How's it going?"

She shrugs. Katy is sort of crabby. Always.

"Can you believe they're talking about cutting so many electives?" I ask. Mrs. J told everyone the bad news during fourth period that day, so the whole newspaper staff knows what's going on. I wave when I see Maleina Madsen, a friend from elementary school. She heads up the steps toward Katy and me. "I can't believe they might stop publishing the paper." I explain the situation as Maleina sits down next to us — since she's not on the paper, she hasn't heard the bad news yet.

Katy looks even more crabby. "My mom said there are some major budget cuts going on all over the school district." She stares at me with this serious look. Katy's mom is on the school board, which means she's always really up on this stuff. "The school board is working on a referendum to get more money for school activities, but it's pretty pointless since no one cares." Katy is also really cynical and super-intense. To put it mildly.

Maleina cuts in. "You might have to stop

publishing the paper? That's terrible!" Her eyes get all wide like a little puppy. Maleina is the opposite of Katy — she's optimistic all the time, but gets really bummed out when she hears sad news, even if it doesn't really affect her. After the *Idol Gives Back* special, she was miserable for weeks.

"Yeah." I glance around the auditorium, watching everyone settle into their seats. Michael Hollings wanders in, joking around with Jeremy Rosenberg. They high-five, then head toward the stage to sit with the rest of the football players. I try to focus. "I need to figure out how to get people excited about the paper again."

"Didn't you just get named editor, Jenna?" Maleina asks.

Katy looks at me with narrow eyes. "You know there can't be an editor if there is no paper, right?"

I nod. "That's why I need to figure out a way to save the paper."

I notice then that Stacey Smith, who is climbing up the bleachers, is holding a copy of my beloved newspaper in her hand. My heart jumps into my throat a little. *If Stacey starts reading the paper, her friends will, and then the sixth graders will, and then . . .*

But just as I start to get excited about the possibility that Stacey Smith and the Seventh Grade Snobs have suddenly taken an interest in the newspaper, Stacey unfolds the paper and places it on the grimy bleacher bench.

Then she sits on it.

My paper is being used as Stacey Smith's seat protector.

I look around and realize that this is happening throughout the room. I don't think I could feel any worse. But then Stacey turns to Jasmine Chen (who is also unfolding a copy of the paper to sit on) and says, "We don't need a school newspaper to tell us what's going on at our school. *I* can tell you what you need to know!"

Jasmine laughs like crazy, but I know Stacey's not joking. She and her friends are the queens of school gossip and decide what everyone needs to know. Unless I can get them interested in my newspaper, I'd better get used to the idea that the *Washington News* will be nothing more than an out-of-date seat protector.

CHAPTER THREE

"Hold the kiwi in this little pocket and squeeze."
My stepmom, Liz, looks at me with such hope that
I can't help but smile at her. "See?" she declares.
"Juice!"

"Got it," I say, watching the juicing machine
with as much enthusiasm as I can muster. "Hold
the fruit in the little hole and push the lever down.
Wow, Liz, that's pretty cool."

She looks at me sharply before noticing the un-
sarcastic smile on my face. "Thanks, Jenna. Your
dad and I really appreciate you helping out." A
little tear bubbles to the corner of her eye. "I
know you'd much rather be hanging out with
your friends on a Saturday afternoon, so the fact
that you're helping us out at Juice It means

22

everything to me. This is going to be such wonderful family time."

"Okay." I raise my eyebrows at her. "Enough now. Don't get all cheeseball on me." Liz is my stepmom, but really, she's a lot more like my *actual* mom than my birth mother ever was. My original parents got divorced when I wasn't even a year old, and my dad got full custody of me. My mom took off and started a different life. I still see her every other Christmas and for a few weeks each summer, but for the most part, it's been me, Dad, and Liz for as long as I can remember.

And, of course, Junior. Stewart Sampson Junior was born three years to the day after me. So now it's the four of us. I always call my dad and Liz my "parents," because it's just easier that way. I totally love Liz, and my real mom is super-happy with her other life. So I guess things worked out for everyone.

"Do you want to try a mango?" Liz asks, pulling a greenish-orangey fruit from the giant fridge. "Give it a squeeze, Jenna."

I take the mango and slice it in half, then cut around the giant pit. I squish the fruit into the juicer and watch as it gets squeezed into gooberey juice. Who would drink this stuff? "I think

I've got the hang of it, Liz. Only a few more minutes until the mall opens — what else do we have to do to get ready?"

Liz looks panicked. "Um," she says nervously, "let me pop in the back room and ask your dad." Then she starts singing this old song, "Don't Worry, Be Happy," as she wanders through the door into the stockroom. She always starts singing weird songs when she's nervous about something.

Today is opening day at Juice It. Our whole family is at the mall, getting things ready. After my parents told me about their strange new venture, they mustered up the nerve to add that I would need to help out with a few shifts at the counter as a Juice Master. I'm not old enough to get a real job, but because this is a family business, my parents can put me to work.

All I can say is, if I'm stuck working at this embarrassing juice bar, I'd better get out of a few of my chores at home. I'll happily give up cleaning my room, thankyouverymuch.

I guess it's not the worst thing in the world, since they are actually paying me in the best possible way. The deal is, if I work three days a week while they get the store up and running, they'll get me a cell phone. I'm totally happy with that. I don't mind hanging out with Liz, and I definitely wouldn't mind having the tools to text my friends.

The only downside is that every other girl in my class hangs out at the mall all the time. I'm sort of embarrassed that I'm there working, not hanging out. It's not like I'm working somewhere cool, like The Edge, which is apparently *the* place to buy clothes. I wouldn't know, but Keisha talks about it all the time. But anyway, I guess things could be worse.

Liz comes out of the back room, and I see this huge pineapple in her hand. I guess we're doing more juicing. She gives me an embarrassed grin, and I start to get nervous. "What?" I say.

"Don't freak out," Liz says. That's a really bad sign. She holds out the pineapple and I take it from her. It's only then that I realize it's not a real piece of fruit, but a stuffed pineapple with a hole in the base.

I'm not stupid. I know what it is.

I lift the pineapple and place it on my head. "It's a hat." I declare blandly. "A pineapple hat." I feel a little sick.

Liz is smiling. Beaming, actually. And, suddenly, she starts laughing. "You look adorable!" She's laughing so hard that she's starting to cry, which makes me want to pull the pineapple off my head and swing it at her. But it's all soft and plushy, so that wouldn't be very effective. "Stew!" she cries, tears of laughter rolling down her face. "Stew, you have to come see how cute Jenna looks!"

My dad emerges from the back room. I know the look on my face is one of horror rather than sunshine and roses, but he, too, cracks up. "It's perfect," he declares.

"Excuse me." I break into their private little laugh party. "What is this?"

"A hat," Junior says, strolling out of the back room with the same style of pineapple hat on his head. He looks ridiculous. I'm tempted to laugh, but know that I look just as crazy, which makes all of this very unfunny. "It's our uniform."

"No." I'm trying to be a good sport. I think a simple no is fairly polite, given the circumstances.

"Yes, Jenna." My dad has stopped laughing and is now holding these ugly aprons in his hand. "We'll all wear these, too." He passes everyone an apron. Mine has lemons printed all over it — they're spilling out of a basket at the top and rolling all the way down to the bottom of the smock. Dad's apron has bananas wearing hats, Junior's is covered in dancing strawberries, and

26

Liz's is decorated with apples carved to look like weird little faces.

My short body is swimming in the apron, and my forehead is completely invisible beneath my pineapple hat. "Dad, this is unnecessary." I'm trying to be rational. In true journalistic form, I want to make sure that we cover all sides of the issue. But as far as I can tell, there are no good sides to this uniform, and I don't plan on wearing it for more than another fourteen seconds. I look like a fool. A fool who is working at the food court at her parents' *juice bar*, for crying out loud.

"Now," my dad says, in full-on father mode, "the mall just opened, so step up to that counter and look happy about it. We're in business!"

Several women come strolling into the food court, and I see them checking out the Juice It menu from afar. They slowly approach the counter and tell me they want two Mango Mangoes. Liz and I work together to put crushed ice, mango, and orange juice into the blender while my dad tries his unique sales pitch on the women. He starts rattling off all sorts of facts about the benefits of fruit in a daily diet, and offers each of them a frozen grape as a sample. He's talking loudly enough that the people at the Wok 'N' Walk are all staring. I want to crawl under the counter.

The pineapple hat is squeezing my head. That's it, I *am* moving to France. "Enjoy," I say, pushing the womens' drinks across the counter.

"A little more oomph!" my dad says to me as the customers walk away. "Let's see the excitement!" My dad gets like this — all crazy excited and over the top. He became more and more goofy after he did infomercials on one of our local cable television channels a few years ago. He's like that guy who sells Orange Glow on cable . . . except he's my dad.

I look at him standing there, all pumped and wild and wearing bananas all over his apron, and I just sort of break down. I mean, I'm almost falling-on-the-floor giggling. Liz and my dad and Junior are all staring at me, and that somehow makes it that much funnier. The pineapple begins to slide off my forehead.

And then, just as soon as I think I might actually die of laughter, I hear a familiar voice — Stacey Smith's voice.

She's coming my way.

CHAPTER FOUR

I hear her before I see her, but there's no doubt in my mind that the voice definitely belongs to the ringleader of the Seventh Grade Snobs, also known as the Fall Carnival Princess. (Michael Hollings and Stacey were named this year's Prince and Princess at assembly — no surprise there.) I can hear Jasmine Chen's nasal, high-pitched, donkey-like laugh interjecting after every other one of Stacey's words.

My own laughing stops. I suddenly drop to the floor, desperate to hide from Stacey and Jasmine.

"Are you having a mental breakdown?" Junior asks plainly. "Because if you are and you have to check into the loony bin, I'm taking your room and your CDs."

"I just dropped something," I respond,

pretending to look on the floor for who-knows-what. "I think I dropped a mango."

My dad and Liz glance at each other, then at me. "Um, Jenna," my dad begins. I shush him, worried Stacey or Jasmine will hear. It's not like they'd recognize my name or anything — there are four hundred kids in our grade, and I'm one of six Jennas — but I'm still worried that they'll see me. It's completely ridiculous, I know that. "Jenna," my dad whispers. "Get up."

I push my hands against the plastic mat that covers the floor, and slowly stand again. Stacey and Jasmine have moved to the other side of the food court, but they're still there. I can hear Stacey loud and clear, even over the din of the mall noise. She's talking about the soccer game they won yesterday, bragging about how "powerful" she was on the field. Ugh.

My dad starts gabbing, preventing me from hearing more. "Jenna," he repeats, "are you okay?" I can see him surveying the food court, checking to see if any potential customers saw my boot camp moves and opted to get fries instead of a smoothie.

"I'm fine," I say. "Can I take a break?" I need five minutes to clear my head, and the idea of squeezing mangoes makes me want to scream.

Also, it suddenly smells like the scented candle section at Bed Bath & Beyond, and given my feelings about fruit . . . well, you can imagine.

My dad furrows his eyebrows. "The store has been open for less than ten minutes. You need a break already?" He looks sort of frustrated, which just makes me mad. "Remember, Jenna, the deal is that we'll get you a cell phone *if* you work three days a week. That's not three five-minute shifts, you know? We all need to pull our weight around here if we want Juice It to be a success."

"Right," I say, trying to remain levelheaded. "I understand. But I just need a few minutes."

Liz is studying me carefully. She says quietly, "Stew, let her go. I've got it covered."

"Five minutes," I promise, shooting Liz a grateful look. I pull my apron and pineapple hat off and push through the swinging door that separates Juice It from the rest of the mall. I walk away from the food court, past Wok 'N' Walk and the chocolate shop, and toward the mall courtyard.

The water fountain in the courtyard smells faintly of chlorine, making me think about the dreaded swimming unit in gym class. The thought makes me cringe. They make us swim a full mile before we can pass seventh grade. It's such a cruel requirement, and there are always horror stories

31

about people who literally spend the whole day trying to finish their mile. Last year, apparently one of the eighth graders at our school, Kristin Langseth, didn't finish until seventh period. And she started swimming during her second-period gym class! That is so going to be me. I try not to think about it.

Despite the pool smell, I decide to sit in the courtyard, resting on one of the benches. I've been there for less than a minute when a guy comes up and sits at the other end of my bench. There are eight benches around the fountain that no one is using, so it's really weird that he's sitting *right* next to me. He's about my age; I think he might go to Washington, but I'm not sure.

"If you think your pineapple hat is bad, you should see what I have to wear after lunch," he says, acting like we're old friends or something.

I narrow my eyes at him, trying to figure out if maybe we do know each other. Then I feel bad. I think I just gave this guy the same look Michael Hollings usually gives me in French class. I know firsthand that it's not a good feeling. "Oh, yeah?" I say. Then I stop, wondering how he knows about my pineapple hat. "How do you know about my pineapple hat?" I ask.

"I work at Moo La La, the ice-cream shop on the other side of the food court. After lunch every day, I stand outside the bookstore wearing either a foam milk-shake costume or a cow suit. I hand out coupons. It's pretty awesome." He slumps back on the bench and grins. "I'm Peter. So this is opening day for the juice bar?"

"Yeah," I respond. I can't help smiling. "I'm Jenna. My parents just opened Juice It today. Do you work for your parents, too?"

Peter nods. "For the last three years. They make me save all the money I make for college, which is not fun."

"Mine promised to get me a cell phone in exchange for working a few days a week. I guess I got a better deal." Never thought I'd say that.

"You did. And like I said, I saw your pineapple hat this morning and I'm still pretty sure that my cow suit is worse. You'll see."

"Does it have udders?"

Peter tilts his head, obviously wondering why I'm asking such a random question. "Yeah. Pink udders," he says finally.

"That doesn't sound too bad, then." I grin at him.

There's something relaxing about the way Peter is lazily slumped on the bench, talking to me like we're already good friends. "You'll have to see for yourself. The costume is the big perk of my job."

"Speaking of which," I say, "I really need to get back to work." I don't want to go back to Juice It. I want to sit here on this bench with Peter all day. He's really nice, and — if I'm being honest — supercute. Not Michael Hollings cute, but still . . . He also made me forget about Stacey Smith and Jasmine Chen for a little bit, which is really saying something. As I stand up, I ask him, "Why aren't you working right now?"

Peter gets up, too, and walks with me. "My shift hasn't started yet, so I was just hanging out until my parents need me. We don't get a lot of morning business for ice cream. But on the weekends, I have to catch a lift with my parents when they come to set up in the morning. Whenever I work after school, I get a ride from my older sister. She got out of working Saturdays by telling my parents she needs the time to study for the SATs."

"Is that true?" I ask.

Peter shrugs. "I'm pretty sure she just has friends over to hang out every Saturday. But the excuse works for her, and I'm not going to ruin it, since I plan to use the same one when I get to high school."

"That sounds like a good idea," I say, laughing. We're almost back at the food court now. I can see my dad serving smoothies to a group of customers. He's wearing a pineapple hat himself now, and he looks ridiculous. He's juggling apples while the customers all laugh. My dad is a total ham. "What school do you go to?" I ask Peter.

"I just transferred from Penn to Washington. We moved to a different house this summer, and it meant switching schools."

"I go to Washington, too!" I say — a little too excitedly. Seriously, I sound like Stacey Smith or something. "What grade are you in?"

"Seventh."

"Me too!" The squeal sneaks out again. I'm totally embarrassed.

"Cool," Peter says. "Well, have fun with the juice. Maybe I'll see you at school sometime." He waves and heads off toward Moo La La.

Peter distracted me from Stacey Smith, so when I get back to Juice It, I'm feeling a lot better. There's also something reassuring about knowing that someone else is in exactly the same shoes as me. But Peter's been working at his parents store for three years, so I guess I can't really complain.

Liz gives me a little kiss on the forehead when I get back, which is sort of embarrassing, but also pretty nice. It feels good to have her care about me so much. As she pulls me into a hug, she whispers quietly, "Everything okay?"

I nod. "I feel better now. Thanks, Liz."

I pop the pineapple hat back on my head and take my turn waiting on a few customers. There are a ton of people buying juice and smoothies from us, and my dad is totally psyched. He starts to clap a few random times, which means he's really pumped about how well things are going.

I notice that Stacey and Jasmine are still sitting in the food court, and whenever I remember to listen, I can hear everything they're saying. Juice It is close to the edge of the food court, and the walls are covered in these little orange glass tiles. I guess the tiles are like little mirrors for sound or something, because I can hear everything as clearly as if Stacey and Jasmine were sitting on the Juice It counter. Which I'm glad they're not.

They talk a lot about the Fall Carnival — which Stacey is super-involved in planning, especially now that she's the Princess — and it's pretty boring until I hear Stacey say, "Dahlia has such a huge crush on Michael Hollings." My ears perk up, eager to catch more of their conversation. "But I heard him tell Christian that he's not into her at all."

Yes! I cheer inwardly. It's not like I think I stand even the tiniest chance with Michael Hollings, but I still don't want him to go out with someone else.

Stacey continues, "And *Christian* . . ." She says his name with this goofy lilt in her voice. "I think he might have a crush on *Dahlia*." I watch her as she talks. She pulls a straw absentmindedly out of the hole in her cup lid, then jabs it back in again. Jasmine watches her every move carefully. A second later, Jasmine tries to pull her straw out of her cup the same way, and I can tell that the drink splashes off the end of her straw because she grabs a napkin and dabs at her shirt and the table.

I listen for almost ten minutes as Stacey rambles on and on about who's crushing on who, and what the other person thinks. I've never been witness to this much gossip in my life. I can't believe she's just saying all of this stuff out in the open at the mall! I thought these people were her friends, but she's obviously not very good at keeping their secrets. If I can hear everything this well, who knows who else is listening in?

Eventually, Stacey slurps up the last of her drink and says, "Ready?"

Jasmine hops off her chair. "For sure!" It's the

37

first thing I've heard Jasmine say all day. Mostly, Stacey has been talking at her. How boring.

Stacey and Jasmine walk right past Juice It on their way out of the food court. Stacey's eyes glaze past me, but I'm pretty sure that the pineapple hat completely masks my appearance. The ridiculous hat could actually come in handy if it means I can hide in the openness of the food court.

Getting to listen in on Stacey Smith and the Seventh Grade Snobs' conversations is a pretty cool perk of my new job. A ton of kids at Washington would pay to hear everything I heard for free.

Stacey and Jasmine really should be careful about where they do their gossiping. They have no idea who might be listening.

CHAPTER FIVE

Michael Hollings and I have never had a conversation in English. In fact, almost all of our conversations have been fully scripted for us by *Bon Voyage!*, our French textbook.

Madame Fishman wrote today's dialogue for us. She passes out a conversation sheet that we're supposed to practice with our partner.

"*Qu'avez–vous fait ce week–end?*" That's Michael, wondering what I did this weekend.

"*Je suis allé au mail.*" My pre-written response is that I went to the mall — how true! "*Qu'avez-vous fait?*"

"*J'ai rendu visite à mes cousins.*" Michael has seriously good pronunciation and sounds like a true French cutie. "*Quelle est votre couleur préférée?*"

"*Pourpre. Font vous aiment des crêpes?*" As we're talking, I can't stop thinking about what Stacey said this weekend — that Dahlia likes Michael. I sneak a glance at my cute partner. His scruffy brown hair is a little longer than usual, and covers his brown eyes a little when he leans forward over his desk. He's all tan from summer baseball practice.

"Hey." That's Michael. I've stopped paying attention to our conversation because I'm distracted by his cuteness. Again. "Are you going to answer the question?" Michael has started speaking in English and gives me this look — sort of amused and curious at the same time. And maybe a little annoyed. He often gives me this look, which makes me suspect that Jenna + Michael will never happen.

"Sorry," I say quietly. "Where were we?"

Michael points to a question about skiing and I recite the answer. Finally, we get to the end of the dialogue sheet and sit there silently, waiting for everyone else to finish. Eventually, Madame Fishman starts talking again, and I am free to zone out without Michael thinking I'm some sort of weirdo.

When the bell rings, I gather my stuff and follow Michael out into the hall. He meets up with

Robbie Prinzo and they do this little hand-slap thing. Then Michael laughs at something Robbie says, and it melts my heart. Why doesn't Michael laugh at anything I say?

I start to make my way to the journalism room, and realize that I will probably only get to hang out in Mrs. J's room during lunch for another few weeks. Then I'll have to start braving the cafeteria. I've been thinking about the newspaper a lot all weekend. I just don't know how I'm going to shake things up so much that people will start reading it.

Keisha catches me as I walk past the center stairs. "Hi, you!" she declares loudly. Michael, who is still walking in front of me with Robbie, turns at the sound of Keisha's voice and gives me a look again.

"How was your game on Friday?" I ask Keisha. I haven't had a chance to talk to her all weekend, since I was at the mall pretty much nonstop, and Keisha had a soccer team dinner at Andra Roy's house on Saturday night.

Keisha raises her fist in the air and cheers, "We won two–nothing!"

"And?" I prompt.

She looks embarrassed, because she knows what I'm getting at. "I scored two, with solid assists from Dahlia." My best friend is so modest.

"You're the star!"

"I didn't say that." She gets all quiet, which is totally rare for Keisha. But when she's forced to brag about herself, she gets really uncomfortable. It's pretty funny, actually. "The team was great."

I nod. "And you were the star. That's all I'm saying."

"So did you come up with any good ideas for saving the paper this weekend?" She quickly changes the subject. "And how was the grand opening?"

"No and good," I state plainly. "The grand opening was a success, I guess." I tell her about the pineapple hat and how the booth stinks like fruit, which makes me want to puke. "The work itself actually wasn't that bad, though, and my dad stayed somewhat in control of his enthusiasm, so he wasn't too embarrassing. But I still have no idea what to do about the paper."

Keisha opens the door to Mrs. J's classroom and sweeps her arm to usher me in. Mrs. J is inside, talking with Mrs. Liu. "Hi, Mrs. Liu," Keisha and I say in unison. We're both surprised to see her there, since the teachers usually go to the main office to meet with the principal, instead of the other way around.

"Hello, girls," Mrs. Liu says seriously. "How was your weekend?"

"Fine," we answer together.

I clear my throat uncomfortably. "Well, Keish, I just need to drop my notebook off and then we can head to the cafeteria."

Keisha looks at me like I'm a lunatic. She knows we never go to the cafeteria, but it's so awkward having Mrs. Liu in the journalism room. I'm dying to get out of there.

Mrs. Liu watches me like a hawk as I drop my newspaper notebook back by the computer. It's obvious that she and Mrs. J are waiting for us to leave. It's silent in the room except for the swishing of my jeans. When I walk past Mrs. Liu, she says, "I understand Mrs. Jensen has told you about our impending budget cuts?"

I'm caught off guard. "Oh — yeah." So she and Mrs. J had been in there talking about the newspaper.

Mrs. Liu smiles this chilly smile and says, "I hope we don't have to take more drastic measures."

"Have a good lunch, girls," Mrs. Jensen says suddenly. She gives me a look that screams, *Get out of here!* I think Mrs. J is secretly a little afraid of Mrs. Liu.

When Keisha and I get to the cafeteria, I immediately remember why I hate eating there. It's crowded, and every table is packed with little groups of friends. Keisha has her soccer friends, and I have some other friends — including a bunch of kids who work on the paper — but neither of us is in a clique. We don't really fit in anywhere.

Keisha and I have been best friends for as long as I can remember. We hung out with Tess Tivenan and Maria Alvarez a lot last year in sixth grade, but they made the cheerleading squad this year and are sort of obsessed. And sometimes we hang out with Maleina Madsen and Katy Gurtzke, but mostly because they live two blocks away from us and we've all known each other for a long time. I like Keisha's soccer friends and everything, but since I have never played on the team, I don't have a lot in common with them. The same goes for Keisha with my newspaper buddies.

I can't help taking a quick look around the room for Peter, the guy from the mall. I'd love to get Keisha's take on him. Scanning, I don't see Peter anywhere, but I do spot Stacey Smith and Dahlia Levine, who both have early lunch, too. Jasmine Chen must be in a different lunch period, since she's nowhere to be seen. The three of them go pretty much everywhere together these days.

The table next to Stacey and Dahlia's is filled with all of the cool guys from our class. Michael Hollings, Jeremy Rosenberg, JJ Stupak, Robbie Prinzo, and their friends. Seeing them reminds me that I haven't told Keisha about all the stuff I overheard on Saturday.

"You're not going to believe what I heard at the mall this weekend!" I whisper.

Keisha looks intrigued. She finds us an empty table back by the windows, and we settle into the only two chairs that aren't broken.

I grin and go on. "Stacey Smith and Jasmine Chen hung out at the food court for almost an hour on Saturday, and they spent the whole time talking about the other Seventh Grade Snobs — and pretty much everyone else at those tables over there." I gesture to the center tables in the lunchroom, where Dahlia is holding her hands over Michael Hollings's eyes. Gag. When she pulls her hands away, I see him giving her the same irritated look he gives me. For once, I'm happy to see it.

"How do you know?" Keisha asks as she chomps into her sandwich. "Could you hear them?"

"Everything." I nod. "They were talking so loud, it was almost like they thought there wasn't anyone else at the mall."

We're interrupted by Katy Gurtzke. "Jenna," she blurts out, standing next to the table. "My mom told me last night that it's not just the newspaper and a few other electives getting cut. The debate team is being cut, too, and a bunch of our sports teams are at risk — everything that doesn't pay for itself through ticket sales or concessions might be on the chopping block." Katy stops to take a breath. "Jenna, we have to cover this story in the newspaper so people know what's happening. The worst part is, it sounds like the Fall Carnival might be getting cut, too. The Carnival is supposed to be a fund-raiser, but we don't even break even since it costs so much to throw."

"Of course we'll cover this story in the paper," I say, still trying to make sense of everything Katy's saying. "Do you want to write the article?"

She nods. "But it's not as if anyone is actually going to *read* the paper, so I don't know how much good it's going to do."

As Katy walks back to her table, I realize it's even *more* important now for me to get people to start reading the newspaper. Oof.

"So what did they say?" As soon as Katy walks away, Keisha quickly shifts the conversation back to the gossip I overheard that weekend. "Earth to Jenna," she says, waving her hand in front of my face. "Stop thinking about the paper for a minute and tell me more about what you heard!"

I start to repeat the things I heard Stacey telling Jasmine at the mall, and the exuberant look on Keisha's face gives me an idea. If Keisha is this interested in school gossip, there must be a ton of people who would love to have a sneak peek into the Seventh Grade Snobs' scoop.

And if you're talking loud enough for someone else to hear you perfectly clearly, then your conversation is open to the world. Right? "Keish!" I announce. "I have an idea!"

"Uh-oh," Keisha groans, setting down her carrot sticks.

"I think I know how I can save the paper," I whisper. "And how I'm going to get people to pay attention to the important issues that we're covering. What if I print the gossip I overhear at the mall? If the gossip column is good enough, everyone at school will read it — and they'll see all of the other news in the paper, too."

"That sounds really risky, Jenna."

"Why?"

"What if Stacey Smith finds out it's you writing the gossip column? She'll kill you." Keisha puts a carrot stick between two chips and eats it like a sandwich.

"I'm not scared of Stacey," I declare confidently . . . much more confidently than I actually feel. "Besides, she's the one talking about her friends' secrets out in the open at the mall. Plus, if I can find a way to save the Fall Carnival, Stacey can't be mad at me."

"I'm sure she wouldn't want to see that get cut any more than you want to see your newspaper get cut," Keisha allows.

I nod. "Exactly. Keish, aren't you a little worried about what Katy told us — that sports might get cut? Do you think soccer's safe?"

Keisha waves her hand dismissively. "I don't believe it," she says. "Katy is such a pessimist. I'm sure she was just being dramatic."

She looks so confident that I almost believe it myself. But as I pick up my garbage, I can't stop a tiny little worry from creeping into my stomach. Katy is usually a really good source of information. What if she's right about everything that's going on? It's my duty as the editor of the

Washington News to make sure everyone has solid facts about what's happening.

A gossip column may be just what I need to get people reading. There's no risk in trying, right?

CHAPTER SIX

"We're ready, we're set, we'll put it in the net! Go Tigers!" I cheer along with the other kids who are hanging out at the soccer game that afternoon. Keisha and her teammates jog onto the field for their scrimmage against West. My parents gave me the afternoon off at Juice It, so I decided to hang out on the sidelines at the game.

I'm sitting with Maleina Madsen, who is cheering louder than anyone. She always does. Maleina desperately wanted to be a cheerleader this year, but got squeezed out by Maria Alvarez, who had the advantage of being able to do two backflips, one after the other.

Now Maleina tries to go to as many school activities as she can, and always cheers super-enthusiastically. I think she's hoping the head cheerleaders will hear her and ask her to join the squad. Unfortunately, the chance of that happening is about as good as me making the soccer team. Let's just say I can't even drooble the ball up the field. (Or is it dribble? See what I mean?)

As we're watching, Stacey sidles up to the captain of the other team and shakes hands. Maleina nudges me and says, "Did you hear about Stacey's party a few weeks ago? Elana Logan told me that they had a professional makeup artist from a *soap opera* come and do everyone's makeup." She sighs, clearly disappointed that she wasn't invited.

I can't help wondering if having my makeup done by some sort of professional would be fun or torture. I guess it would be pretty cool to see what I'd look like all glammed up, but I'd be nervous they'd poke me in the eye with their equipment. And skin products always smell all fruity, which — obviously — is not great for me.

"Stacey always seems like she has so much fun." Maleina sighs. "Don't you wish you could hang out with her and her friends sometime, just to see what it's like?"

"I guess," I say. I *have* always wanted to know what it would be like to hang out with the Seventh

Grade Snobs. I don't necessarily want to be friends with them or be like them, but it would be cool to know a little more about what's going on in our class — and they know everything. And, of course, I'd love to see what Michael is like when he's not being all quiet and mysterious in French class. *Oui, oui.*

A soccer ball sails my way, and as I throw it back toward the field, I notice that Michael Hollings and a few of his friends are walking up. Dahlia Levine spots them at the same time as I do, and forgets to keep her eye on the game. A pass that was intended for her sails through the side-lines and rolls over to Michael. He kicks the ball back onto the field and shouts, "Nice one, Dahlia!" while his friends all laugh.

I can see Dahlia's face turn red, and I suddenly feel bad for her. If she really does have a crush on Michael, that move would have been so embarrassing! Michael and his friends sit in the stands near me, and I spend the rest of the first half of the game listening to them making fun of some of the girls on the team. I think they're just trying to be funny, but some of the stuff they're saying is kind of mean. Boys.

At halftime, Dahlia and Stacey both come over to joke around with the guys. It seems like they all get along pretty well, so I guess I just don't really understand seventh grade guys . . . Michael Hollings, in particular (surprise, surprise!).

Maleina heads off to say hi to some of the cheerleaders. I know she just wants to get close enough that they can hear her exceptional cheering.

"Hey!" Keisha bellows, as she climbs up the stands toward me. "What'd you think of the first half?"

I can't admit that I was barely paying attention, so I just say, "Great job out there!"

She gestures toward Michael, who is now sitting next to Dahlia. Stacey is looking on proudly, like Little Miss Matchmaker. "Are they going out?" Keisha whispers.

I shrug.

"You okay?" Keisha wipes some sweat off her forehead and gives me this sort of pitying look.

"It's not like I thought I had a chance with him or anything. I'm not totally crazy." But that doesn't make me feel any better. Watching Michael and Dahlia flirt, there's a giant rock of jealousy in the bottom of my stomach that makes me want to puke. I didn't think I'd ever really care about whether I was popular or not, but today I can't help but wonder — *if I were as popular as Stacey and Dahlia, could that be me?*

After the soccer game, Keisha and I walk to her house. My parents are both at the mall until it closes, so Keisha's mom invited me over for dinner. Poor Junior has to have Wok 'N' Walk.

"Keish, listen . . . that stuff Katy was telling us about sports getting cut? Well, it's real."

"What do you mean?" Keisha switches her soccer bag from one shoulder to the other. It looks heavy and makes me feel lucky that journalism doesn't involve such heavy equipment.

"I did some research before the game, and it looks like every school in our district has to find a way to save money this year. They've been told to cut electives first, and then move on to other activities." I hold out my hand and offer to take her bag. She looks so tired after the game.

When I have the bag squarely on my shoulder, I continue. "Katy was also right about the Fall Carnival — they're probably going to have to cut it. And if all that doesn't save enough money, they're talking about only continuing two fall sports — football and cheerleading, since they're the most popular. They might have to cut your team after this season."

Keisha's quiet, listening. She knows that I've done my research. I don't jump to conclusions — a good reporter has all the facts — so when I say this is bad, she knows it's bad. "What can we do?" she asks finally.

"There are a couple of options. The easiest would be to just hope for the best."

Keisha looks at me like I'm crazy. "As if you're going to just let the newspaper go down without a fight. And there's no way I'm going to practice as hard as I did this summer and let this be the last year of soccer."

"That's what I thought," I say. "So the other option is to use the newspaper to get the word out." As I list the things that need to happen, I'm starting to feel majorly overwhelmed. It seemed hopeless when I just needed to save the newspaper, but now that I know there are a ton of programs at risk, I'm sort of freaking out. And I have to save the newspaper before I can help save the other activities.

Keisha takes her bag back and slings it over her shoulder. I'm relieved, since it literally felt like I was carrying a small person over my arm. Junior doesn't weigh as much as Keisha's soccer bag.

"I don't know how the newspaper is going to help," Keisha suddenly blurts out. "Jenna, no one reads it."

"That's where my new gossip column will be our friend and ally!" I exclaim as we climb the steps up to Keisha's house.

"You still think that crazy idea is a good plan?"

"I do. But I need your help."

"Nuh-uh," Keisha says, shaking her head and frowning. "I don't want to be a part of this."

"One little favor?"

She sighs. "What?"

"I just need you to steal a few of your sisters' celebrity magazines." Keisha's sisters are both in high school, and are completely obsessed with Hollywood and celebrities and gossip. They're so different from Keisha — Kendra is a singer (she's auditioned for *American Idol* twice!) and Claudia is an actress.

"Why?" Keisha looks suspicious. "Are you going to write about Lindsay Lohan in our school's gossip column?"

"I don't actually know how to write a gossip column," I admit. "I'm afraid what I write will be a little too newspaper-y to get the job done. So I need to study."

"Study *Us Weekly* and *Star* and *In Touch*?"

"Yep." I smile. "I need to make Stacey Smith and the Seventh Grade Snobs' scoop sound as exciting as *Us Weekly* would . . . or it will be pretty obvious who's writing my anonymous column."

Keisha rolls her eyes. "We have a lot of work to do."

"You'll help me?"

"I'll help," Keisha reluctantly agrees. "But I still think this is risky, Jen."

"What could go wrong? It's a perfect plan."

"There is no such thing, Jenna." Keisha looks at me firmly before pushing the door to her house open. "And *that's* why I'm nervous."

CHAPTER SEVEN

JUICY GOSSIP
by Little Miss Mango

Leave it to a certain group of pretty and popular seventh grade girls to give us plenty to gab about. . . .

★ Rumor has it that one popular, ponytailed blond girl has a crush on a certain someone. And that certain someone (who plays third base on the Washington baseball team) has his eye on someone else. The best part is that there's a third player in the mix . . . and he likes Ponytail Girl. Who will end up with the blond cutie?

★ Did anyone miss the small, uh, incident last week that resulted in a certain red-haired someone leaving the cafeteria in tears? Girl, you really should make sure your wrap skirt is planning to stay wrapped before you go out in public!

★ Apparently, a very special birthday party is coming up ... and there are several people who may not have made the guest list. Will they still get the birthday girl a present, or is this the end of those friendships? Stay tuned.

★ The captain of the girls' soccer team was overheard gabbing about her friends — some of whom she calls "boring." Scandalous!

I set down the paper midway through reading my first edition of "Juicy Gossip." I was able to include a few snippets about people in the sixth and eighth grades, since I hear a lot from my post at the mall, but it's mostly focused on the seventh grade. I feel a little bad about how much info I revealed, but it's all for a good cause, right?

And the best part? I'm sitting in the bleachers during our weekly assembly, and the gym is almost silent. Almost everyone in the room is holding a copy of the paper, devouring "Juicy Gossip." The article about the school board's funding cuts is in this week's paper, too. So as soon as people get through "Juicy Gossip," they'll move on to the other stories in the paper. (This is how I convinced Mrs. J to let me print "Juicy Gossip" in the first place!) And then they'll be well-informed about the funding cuts, and I'll have a well-read paper. It's a perfect crime.

But a few minutes later, I discover I am wrong, wrong, wrong. People finish reading the gossip and immediately turn to their friends to talk about it. No one is reading the rest of the paper! It's like the other pages don't even exist.

"Jenna!" Keisha storms up the bleachers. She looks angry, and is extra-loud when she yells my name. A few other seventh graders turn to stare at me. "Jenna," Keisha says, sitting next to me and switching over to a whisper. "How could you write all of that?"

Moi? I respond coyly. "I didn't write it."

Keisha is the only person who knows that isn't true. "Jenna, it's a lot worse than I thought it was going to be!"

"But look," I defend myself. "Everyone is reading the paper now!"

"They're reading 'Juicy Gossip.' They're reading about our classmates. They're not reading the rest of the paper at all."

I know she's right. The guilty pit starts to

form in my stomach again. Do I want to save my newspaper if it's not really a *news*paper anymore?

At that moment, Stacey Smith and her friends come gliding into the gym, each of them holding a copy of the *Washington News*. I can't tell if they look upset, but I definitely get a little nervous when they scan the bleachers. Do they know it's me writing "Juicy Gossip"?

"Stacey!" Robbie Prinzo shouts. "Did you read the school newspaper? You're a celebrity!"

Stacey sweeps her silky hair away from her face and smiles calmly at Robbie. "I already knew that."

Keisha and I watch Stacey and her friends slide into the bleachers a few rows below us. Stacey turns to Jasmine. "I *have* to figure out who wrote 'Juicy Gossip.' What kind of name is Little Miss Mango, anyway?"

I can't help but grin. I'm proud of the title of my gossip column and my pen name. They're pretty appropriate, since I overheard all of the scoop while I was working at Juice It. No one will ever make the connection, since they don't even know I work there. It's pretty clever, if I do say so myself.

Jasmine Chen opens her copy of the paper. "I can't believe how much Little Miss Mango wrote about us!"

"I want to write for the paper," Dahlia says. "It's pretty cool."

Whoa! The paper is cool?

"Whatever," Stacey says, pulling her hair into a twisty ponytail at the base of her neck.

Jasmine and Dahlia glance at each other. "Whatever? Stace, the paper is full of scoop about *us*. They called me a blond cutie!" Dahlia giggles. "How can it *not* be cool?"

"It also had some pretty bad stuff about us," Stacey says.

"Yeah," Jasmine echoes. "Like that Stacey's been calling her friends boring? And we know that's not true. We have to find out who Little Miss Mango is! I bet it's Elana. She's probably mad she's not invited to my birthday party."

"It's not Elana, Jasmine," Stacey says dismissively. "Why would Elana write about *herself*? She's the one who lost her wrap skirt last week, remember?"

Jasmine pauses for a minute. "Oh, sorry — is that a bad idea? Sorry if I'm *boring* you, Stacey." She twists her long bangs around her finger.

Uh-oh. They're fighting because of my column? Yeeps.

Stacey sighs. "I didn't say that, Jasmine. Come on, are you going to trust a gossip column to tell you what I think? All I was saying is that Elana probably wouldn't want more people to know about her wrap skirt accident."

"That's a good point," Jasmine says reluctantly. "But who else knows all of that stuff?"

Stacey unfolds her copy of the *Washington News* and stares down at "Juicy Gossip." "I don't know, but I'm going to find out."

"Hi." I jump a little at the sound of a familiar voice right behind me as I gather stuff from my locker after seventh period that day. I turn to see a river of shiny, straight hair and the glimmer of Stacey Smith's lip gloss. I'm the only other person around, so she's obviously talking to me — even though this is literally the first time Stacey's uttered a single word to me. "Jenna, right?"

"Yeah," I respond. My voice is sort of crackly.

"I read the new column in the newspaper," Stacey says. "You're the editor, right?"

"Of the paper?"

Stacey looks at me like I'm dumb. "No, editor of the math team," she mocks.

I laugh uncomfortably. "Oh. Yeah."

"So . . ." She pushes her lips out in a little pout. "Are you gonna tell me who Little Miss Mango is?"

My whole body tenses up. She definitely has no idea that I'm the one writing the gossip column. "Oh, w-well," I stammer, "that's confidential. We have to protect our writer's privacy."

"Are you serious?"

I nod. "It's an anonymously written column."

Stacey is clearly unaccustomed to hearing no. "But your writer is writing about me and my friends!" She's starting to get angry. "I deserve to know!"

"Sorry." I shrug. I feel a lump of guilt rising in my throat.

"It's not cool to gossip about someone like that!" she declares.

She's one to talk.

"I can't tell you who the writer is," I say again.

"That's okay." Stacey suddenly smiles. It's this weird, forced smile and it makes me uncomfortable. "I understand."

I stare at her. "You do?" I'm pretty sure she's just trying to be nice to get something out of me.

"Sure." She twirls the combination on her locker and grabs her backpack. "Are you walking out?"

"Uh, yeah." I had been waiting for Keisha, but I sort of forget about that.

"Yeah?" She walks toward the center stairs, then turns to look back at me.

I realize she's waiting for me to walk out with her. Keisha is late, so I wonder if maybe she's not meeting me. "Okay," I say, slamming my locker shut. I forget to grab my French workbook, but I don't bother going back for it. Stacey Smith is waiting to walk out with me. I know she's probably just trying to get on my good side so I'll talk about the source of "Juicy Gossip," but at the moment, I don't really care. This is my chance to get a glimpse into the inner workings of the Seventh Grade Snobs!

Stacey swings her bag over a shoulder and heads down the stairs. "So, do you like working on the paper?"

"Yeah," I say quietly. "I really do."

"That's cool," Stacey says, which surprises me. The paper has never been cool before, and it's weird that it suddenly seems like it is . . . because of "Juicy Gossip."

We don't say anything else as we walk, but I sort of feel like I'm walking in this happy glow or something. It's almost like we're friends — which I know we're not. Stacey is the leader of the Seventh

65

Grade Snobs, and I am the editor of the school newspaper. Those are two totally different universes at Washington. But even though we're not friends, I'm getting a little glimpse into what it would feel like to be popular.

We pass Michael Hollings in the hall. He shoots this coy little grin at Stacey, then turns to look at me with the same smile on his face. It almost feels like I've been a wriggly little caterpillar inside a hairy cocoon for the first few weeks of school, and suddenly I'm this big, purple butterfly or something.

Okay, that's totally cheesy-sounding, but seriously — I don't think Michael has ever looked at me like that! And he just did because I'm with Stacey Smith!

This all feels strange. *Good* strange.

When we get outside, Stacey waves to Jasmine and Dahlia, who are waiting for her right outside the gym doors. "See you later, Jenna." She flips her hand in a little wave at me as she walks off.

"Bye," I call quietly after her. When I look up a few seconds later, Stacey and her friends are gone. But Keisha is standing in their place.

She walks over. "I thought you were waiting for me. But you ditched me to walk out with Stacey?"

I try to explain, but find the words all jumbling

together in my throat. I don't really know why I left without Keisha, so I finally just say, "Sorry, Keish. I'm really sorry I ditched you — I guess I just got caught up."

"Yeah, you did."

We walk the rest of the way home in silence. There is no worse feeling in the world than your best friend being mad at you. Believe me.

CHAPTER EIGHT

The next day at school, things get even stranger. It's almost like I've suddenly started wearing just the right jeans or something (which I haven't), because I've gone from invisible to visible overnight.

When Keisha and I walked into school that morning, every copy of the *Washington News* was gone from the newspaper racks near the main doors. People were standing around in the halls in little groups, reading *my* newspaper. A few guys I sort of know from my sixth period English class gave me high fives as I passed them in the hall. It was kind of embarrassing when my hand made a *pat-pat-pat* sound against theirs instead of a solid *slap*.

In first period math class, I can feel people

watching me as I walk into the room. I hear a few people whispering about some of the gossip from the paper. I'm pretty sure I even hear someone say that they're trying to get up the nerve to ask me if they can write for the paper.

It's almost like I'm suddenly some sort of school celebrity, all because I'm the editor of the once-lame-now-cool paper. I feel like I'm on display . . . which might be a problem, since I'm wearing an outfit my grandma bought me this summer when I visited her in Wisconsin. I never thought I'd worry about what it looks like, but now I'm questioning its cool factor.

Keisha and I have second period gym class together, and by the time we change and sit along the wall of the gym a few minutes before class, at least fifty people have said hi to me since the beginning of the school day. Kids who have never even looked at me before ask me how I'm doing, and Jeremy Rosenberg even moves his feet out of the way when I pass him in the gym.

"This is weird." Keisha vocalizes my exact thoughts. I sort of don't want to jinx it by saying anything.

"Yeah," I echo.

"Who would have guessed that a simple little gossip column would turn *you* into an overnight celebrity?" Keisha leans toward me, trying to keep Katherine Szuchman from hearing our conversation. We're setting up the volleyball nets in the gym, and Katherine is trying to listen in. Katherine is sort of famous as the school's eavesdropper and blabbermouth. She's never tried listening to me and Keisha before, but suddenly it seems like what we have to say is worth overhearing. I would say it's really annoying, but realize I'm doing the same thing at the mall to get my scoop for "Juicy Gossip." Gulp — Katherine Szuchman and I have something terrible in common!

Keisha nudges me. "Jenna, don't you think this is weird? Stacey Smith hanging out with you yesterday, everyone giving you high fives and saying hi to you today, Katherine suddenly interested in our conversation . . . it's strange."

I can't tell if she's upset, but the tone of her voice is sort of off. "I didn't plan this," I whisper, a little more defensively than I meant to. "I thought 'Juicy Gossip' would just get more people to read the paper. I didn't think anyone even knew I was the newspaper editor. I never would have guessed anyone would pay attention to *me!*"

"Well, they are," Keisha says. "Stacey Smith is." There's a definite edge to her voice now. Katherine throws a ball in our direction and chases after it. I'm pretty sure she just wants to get closer, to hear what we're whispering about. "Your plan to save the newspaper seems to be working. People love it now. They love you." She doesn't mean this in a good way — it sounds sort of bitter.

Just then, Coach Roy blows her whistle and we both get quiet. I spend the rest of class thinking about what Keisha said, which means I get beaned in the head with the ball more than the normal amount of times. I know Keisha is upset with me for what happened after school yesterday, but it seems like there's more to it than that.

After we change back into our regular clothes, Keisha and I walk through the hall together. We don't say anything, even when I stop at her locker so she can grab her books for third period. Then she follows me to my locker, which is on her way to class. As I spin the combination, I can't hold it in any longer.

"Are you jealous that Stacey Smith is paying attention to me?" I blurt out.

Keisha narrows her eyes at me, but doesn't say anything. I don't really know how to read her when she doesn't talk. So I just continue, "That's ridiculous, you know! Stacey was only talking to me because she wants to know who Little Miss Mango is." As I say it, I realize that's probably the truth.

Keisha snorts a little and says, "That doesn't bother you?"

The truth is, I'm not psyched about it. But I don't hate the sudden transformation from nobody to somebody — it makes me feel like my work on the paper will finally be worth something, at least. "Not really," I say in response to Keisha's question. "If people are reading the paper, I'm doing my job. And I have better access to the gossip at school by hanging out with Stacey. You know I'm just doing all of this to help save our school activities, right?"

Before I can tell her that this won't affect our friendship and that she means more to me than any of this, Keisha mutters something about being late and walks away. I figure I'll see her in an hour at lunch, anyway, and don't really worry about it.

We've never had a fight before. Actually, that's not true. We had one fight, but it was really silly. We were six and driving to the pool with Keisha's mom. I kept calling this bracelet that Keisha was wearing blue, and she was convinced it was green, and it became this huge deal. I think it was technically teal, so I guess we were both right, but that's totally beside the point. I'm sure Keisha's not mad at me or anything now — I mean, how can she be? What did I do wrong?

By the time I find my workbook at the bottom of my locker, I'm forced to hustle, because I'm late for French class. When I walk into Madame Fishman's room, people are already sitting with their partners, practicing the day's conversation sheet. Madame Fishman checks the clock and gives me a look, but doesn't say anything since I'm never late. "*Merci*, Madame," I say as I pass her desk.

Plunking down in my seat, I brace myself for Michael's cold gaze. But when I turn to him to apologize for being late, he's *smiling* at me. My heart starts pattering in my chest, sort of freaking out. Michael Hollings is smiling at me — for the second time in less than twenty-four hours!

"*Bon jour,*" Michael says. "*J'adore croissants.*"

Okay, I'm totally making up the "*j'adore crois-sants*" part. But he did just say "*bon jour*" to me. In a friendly kind of way.

"Hi, Michael," I say in response. My French phrases have completely slipped my mind. All I can think about is how his eyes resemble fresh-baked brownies. They're so deep and chocolatey and warm looking.

73

"It's cool that you edit the school paper," he says in English. "Way cool."

"Oh. Thanks."

That's the end of our conversation. We turn to the conversation sheet and start speaking in French about farm animals or something, but it doesn't matter. Michael Hollings and I just had a conversation! A real conversation that wasn't scripted for us by Madame Fishman or *Bon Voyage*! This is big.

I am in a daze through the rest of class, singing the same little song over and over in my head: *Michael Hollings talked to me, Michael Hollings talked to me, Michael Hollings talked to meeeeeeeee. . . .*

By the time the bell rings, the voice in my head is sort of hoarse. I stand up with the rest of the class and float out into the hall. When I get to my locker, I push my French workbook into the back with all my sticky notes and pull out my bagel sandwich and chips.

Ever since our encounter with Mrs. Liu, I haven't been going to Mrs. J's room during lunch. I wait for Keisha by my locker. After about five minutes, I start to get a little nervous that she may not be coming. Keisha and I almost always eat lunch together. What do I do now?

"Hi, Jenna." Stacey Smith's voice startles me so much that I slam my locker door closed.

"Oh," I say, pretending to be all casual and comfortable around her. Nice try. "How's it going, Stacey?" I pull at my sweater.

Stacey smiles, smacking her glossy lips together. "Are you going to the caf for lunch?"

The caf. As though it's a cool place to hang out. *The caf.* "Um, yeah, I guess." I wasn't planning to go to the cafeteria by myself, but Stacey will think I'm some sort of major loser if I say no. If Keisha didn't show up in the next two minutes, I was going to go to the library.

But who spends their lunch period in the library?

"Great!" Stacey says, smiling again. "Do you want to sit with me?"

My eyes get big. I've just been invited to sit at the Seventh Grade Snobs' table. Me. Jenna Sampson. Formerly invisible editor of the school newspaper.

"So?" Stacey says, looking at me with one arched eyebrow. I don't know how she does that. I can only lift both eyebrows together, which just makes me look sort of surprised. Or like an owl. Either way, it's not right.

I look both ways down the hall for Keisha.

It seems like she's definitely not going to show up, so I figure it can't hurt to go to the "caf" with Stacey. Plus, I don't think Stacey invites new people to her table very often, and I'm *sure* no one has ever said no before. At least this way I don't have to hide out in the library. "Um, sure."

"Cool."

"Yeah," I echo. "Cool." But I don't feel cool. I know she's just being nice to get information out of me about "Juicy Gossip." I feel really weird walking to the cafeteria with Stacey. And I miss my best friend.

"What did you do last night, Jenna?" Stacey asks as we head down the back stairs.

I was at the mall, working at Juice It. But I can't blow my cover yet. I need a lot more scoop for next week's "Juicy Gossip." "Not much. I worked on my French homework a little bit." Total lie. I forgot my French workbook in my locker yesterday. But she doesn't know that.

"That's cool," Stacey says. "I take French, too. We should hang out sometime and work on it together."

"Okay," I say, stunned. I don't know what else to say to her, and I'm sure things are only going to get worse once Dahlia and Michael and everyone

76

else at lunch is around. I am not prepared for this sort of thing.

Keisha would know exactly what to do in this situation. Do I try to talk? Or do I just sit there, laughing at Stacey's jokes?

Where is Keisha when I need her more than I ever have before?

Stacey walks into the cafeteria, and I follow a few steps behind her. I can see people at other tables watching us, wondering why I'm following Stacey Smith to the center table in the "caf." But no one says anything. Stacey turns to smile at me as we walk to the center of the room, which makes me feel a little better about being there. A *little*.

Elana Logan looks at me curiously when I sit down, but she doesn't say hi. She sort of pushes her lips out into this little pout, and I wonder if that's some secret signal or something. When she's not looking, I try to do the same thing with my lips, but immediately stop and vow to try it at home in the mirror before embarrassing myself in public.

No one really says anything to me, so I just sit quietly, chewing my sandwich and part of a giant cookie that Stacey bought for everyone to share. I listen while they talk about Stacey's new jeans and Dahlia's puppy. They're all really excited about some new TV show that just started, and I make a mental note to watch it next time it's on. Even though I'm not exactly having fun, I'm suddenly feeling a little more in-the-know — after just one lunch!

My heart skips a few beats when JJ Stupak scoots his chair over to our table. For a minute, I think that maybe Michael will come over, too, but he stays at the guys' table, joking around. I catch him looking at me a few times, and wonder if maybe I was right about him paying more attention to the popular girls. He definitely notices me more now that Stacey and I are hanging out. Or maybe he's just wondering what in the world I'm doing at this table. That seems more likely.

Toward the end of lunch, Stacey starts talking about Fall Carnival. She wants everyone's opinion on what she should wear for her Princess outfit. I start to say something about the budget cuts, to tell them that the Fall Carnival might be canceled, but I know it makes me sound sort of dorky. I mean, I haven't said anything all through lunch, and suddenly I'm talking about budget cuts? Boring.

So instead, I stuff a chunk of cookie in my mouth. I'm just here to listen. How else will I find out what it's like to be a Seventh Grade Snob?

CHAPTER NINE

"Moo La Laaaaah!" A guy in a cow suit shimmies around the mall corridor, plushy udders swinging with each hop. "Moo la laaaaaah!" When he spins around, I see that it's Peter.

"Hi, Peter." I wave, noticing that the cow suit is just as embarrassing as he said . . . but also kind of cute. On Peter, anyway. I'm walking with Liz toward the food court on Saturday afternoon — my dad gave us both the morning off. Business has been really good, so he hired our first non-family employee. Dad was training him this morning, and asked Liz and I to come in for the afternoon shift.

"Hey, there!" Peter lifts a hoof.

Liz gives me this sappy look and wiggles her eyebrows, like, *Who's* this *guy?* then whispers that she'll meet me at Juice It. I roll my eyes at her, since it's not like that. Peter is a *friend*. Not even. We just met.

As Liz walks away, Peter crosses over to me. "Want a coupon for a milk shake?"

I wrinkle my nose. "Um, no, thanks. Icy drinks make me a little sick these days."

"I get it," Peter says, laughing. "Does that mean you're not taking advantage of the free smoothies during your shift?"

"Fruit freaks me out."

Peter unzips the cow costume to his waist, revealing a black T-shirt with a crossword puzzle on it. He starts to walk toward the food court with me. The cow costume's bulky fabric forces him to waddle, which makes him look even more ridiculous. "Fruit freaks you out?"

"It's weird, I know."

"Not weird," Peter says. Then he pauses. "Okay, maybe a little weird."

I laugh. "I guess so." I gesture to his shirt. "Do you like crossword puzzles?" I *love* crossword puzzles, but am always a little embarrassed to admit it.

"Uh-huh," Peter says, clearly unashamed. "I love them." I am getting this zingy little feeling in my fingers and toes, and start to wonder if maybe

Peter has something to do with it. But just then, I spot Michael Hollings coming out of The Shoe Dude with Robbie Prinzo. My natural instinct is to hide, until I remember our conversation yesterday afternoon in French.

Peter cuts into my thoughts. "How have you been, anyway? I haven't seen you since last weekend."

Michael Hollings is coming closer. The zingy feeling in my fingers and toes has morphed into numbness. "Oh, um," I say, trying to pay attention to Peter but completely distracted by Michael. "I worked on Thursday."

"Oh, yeah?" Peter says. "So how's it going?"

I pat my hair. Michael is only a few steps away. I can't stop myself and suddenly blurt out, "Hi, Michael."

Michael looks up. His head nods very slightly — so slightly, in fact, that he might have just ignored me completely. My stomach drops when he keeps walking without saying anything.

"Is that your friend?" Peter glances at Michael, then adds with a laugh, "He seems nice." I can't tell if he's making fun of me.

All the blood in my body rushes to my face. I've just made a total fool out of myself — and

Peter saw the whole thing. "Yeah," I stammer. "We're partners in French class."

"I thought he looked familiar," Peter says. "I think his locker is near mine."

I'm still queasy, but try to shake it off to pay attention to Peter.

"Oh." That's all I can muster. I sort of want to throw up.

We've finally made it all the way to the food court, and Peter turns toward Moo La La. He waves. "Later, Jenna."

"Bye." I plan to crawl under the Juice It counter for the next few years.

"Hey!" He calls back over his shoulder. One of his hands is holding the unzipped top of the cow costume around his waist. His legs are still covered in white-and-black spotted material. "What lunch do you have?"

"Early lunch."

Peter nods. "I figured that's why I haven't seen you." Has he been looking for me at school? "I have late lunch. Keep an eye out for me this week in the hall, okay? If you say hi, I promise I'll say hey back." Then he smiles this dopey little grin and trots off toward Moo La La.

The whole time I'm changing into my apron, my brain is working overtime. Why did Michael act like he hardly knows me? I can't believe I actually said hi. I feel like an idiot.

And I was humiliated in front of Peter. We could be friends, but after Michael totally ignored me, Peter will probably realize that I'm a huge dork and stay far away from me forever.

This is going to be a bad day.

Grumpily, I put my pineapple on my head and make my way out of the back room. There's a long line at the counter. My dad is chatting with a couple of ladies who have ordered Mango Mangoes. His apron is tied around his waist, and on top he's wearing one of those T-shirts with a fake bare-chested man's body on it. I'm not even kidding — my dad is humiliating. If anyone from school saw me right now, I'd be stuck in social Siberia forever. Thank goodness Dad's not showing his real stomach. That would be gross.

Liz is whipping up a Strawberry Samba, pretending that she doesn't see my dad. But since she's shaking with laughter behind the industrial-size blender, I know she sees him. She always thinks he is *so* funny. At least someone does.

Junior grins at me from his post at the juicing station, then cradles his pineapple hat in his arm like a baby and pretends to feed it a slice of mango that he's cut into the shape of a bottle.

Why is this my family? Life is so unfair.

I have no interest in dealing with people right now, so I offer to help Liz make drinks behind the scenes. She gladly accepts, and we stand side by side, dumping ice and yogurt methodically into our blenders.

The worst part about my exchange with Michael this morning was how horrible it felt to be invisible again. I was still riding so high from my day yesterday — lunch with Stacey and her friends was actually okay. Even though I didn't really say anything, I got that same glowing feeling I had when I'd walked out of school with Stacey. It was sort of nice to be on the inside, for once.

All through lunch, though, I kept wishing that Keisha could have been with me. I know she won't take my word for it that the Seventh Grade Snobs aren't as snobby as I've always thought. Keisha knows Stacey and Dahlia from soccer, but I'm sure it would be so different if she hung out with them outside of the team.

But more than that, I *missed* Keisha yesterday. When I bumped into her after school, I found out she got stuck in third period helping Mrs. Andrews clean up the science lab after Jeremy Rosenberg's experiment caused a major disaster. She didn't seem angry with me anymore, but I can't help feeling a little sick about our conversation yesterday.

After about ten minutes of juicing in silence, Liz turns to look at me. "You okay?"

"Fine," I say, a little more snappily than I meant to.

"Okay, okay." She laughs a little before turning back to her smoothie machine. Liz never gets crabby when I'm snappy with her, which I love. I always know I can talk to her no matter what mood I'm in.

"I guess I just don't want to talk about it, is all," I say. "I'm having sort of a bad day." The vision of Michael staring at me blankly flashes through my head.

"Got it. But let me know if you do want to talk, okay?" Liz gives me her very serious parent look.

I nod, and she gives me a quick kiss on the cheek before making her way out into the food court for her break. My dad is still busy charming people at the counter, and Junior has made himself a little seat *under* the counter, where he's now reading a comic book. Junior is only nine, and they can't really expect him to be that much help. He has a pretty good attitude about helping out at Juice It, considering.

I'm sort of mindlessly squeezing oranges when I hear Jasmine Chen's nasal laugh. I lift my head, and see her, Stacey, and Dahlia standing together at the Juice It counter, ordering drinks.

I panic for a second, before realizing that they're not paying any attention to me. I pull my pineapple hat down lower on my forehead and mix up the drinks they ordered — a Blueberry Morning smoothie, a papaya-mango juice, and a pineapple-banana freeze. My dad pushes them across the counter to Stacey and her friends, after reciting a little poem about blueberries. Through the whole thing, they never notice me behind the blenders. As ugly and embarrassing as it is, my pineapple hat is a pretty good disguise, I guess.

When Stacey and her friends walk away from the counter, I can still hear their conversation clearly. Just like last weekend, they spend the next forty-five minutes in the food court going on and on about their friends. They talk about how Dahlia's crush on Michael is going nowhere, gab a little about Jasmine's party, and talk about stuff that happened to their other friends at school this week.

By the time they slurp up the last drops of their drinks, the next issue of "Juicy Gossip" is pretty much already written in my head.

CHAPTER TEN

"Jenna, I have some news." Mrs. Jensen touches my arm as I pass her in the hall before second period on Monday. "Can you come by the journalism room during your lunch break?"

"Sure, Mrs. J," I say. I wish she'd just tell me whatever it is now, since it must have something to do with the newspaper. She never refers to her room as the "journalism room" unless we're talking about the paper. She's probably going to tell me this week's issue of the newspaper is going to be the last, and I hate waiting for bad news.

When I get to gym class, I stall a little longer than usual, waiting for Keisha to change into her swimsuit. We just switched to our swimming unit. Our mile swim is at the end of the month, and I'm totally dreading it.

Keisha and I grab our towels and head up the stairs to the pool deck. We haven't really talked since last week, when things were weird between us. I was at Juice It pretty much the whole weekend, so we didn't get to hang out at all. I've never gone this long without talking to my best friend.

"Keisha, are you mad at me?" I finally say, unable to stand it any longer.

Keisha looks at me. "I was. A little bit."

"Why?" I ask quietly. "Are you upset that I'm hanging out with Stacey and her friends?"

"I wouldn't care if you were just hanging out with them, Jenna — but you ditched me last week to be with Stacey. You just seem sort of different with all of this popularity and 'Juicy Gossip.' I don't know."

We step onto the pool deck, and Katherine Szuchman scoots close to us as we sit and dangle our feet in the water. Keisha and I look at each other and crack up — Katherine is so obvious! I whisper, "I'm sorry if I've been acting weird!" I can't stop myself from giving Keisha a big hug. This is not normal (especially since we're wearing bathing suits), and she knows it.

"All right," she says, a little suspicious. "I guess everything was strange last week, which is probably why you're acting like a total kook right now."

She grins. We each get up to grab a kickboard, then head back to the pool edge. "I have to tell you something important, but not here. How was your weekend at the mall?"

"Keish, that's not fair!" I declare, but she gestures toward Katherine. Now I have to wait for Mrs. J's news, *and* whatever Keisha has to tell me!

We slide into the water, and between laps I fill Keisha in on Juice It, artfully leaving out the part about overhearing more of Stacey's gossip. I know she'd be curious, but it's also really clear that she doesn't approve of me writing "Juicy Gossip." So I'm not even going to mention that I'm planning to write my column again this week.

With ten minutes left in second period, we're dismissed from the pool. It's a mad dash to shower and get dressed. I did *not* luck out, getting stuck with second period gym class. The kids who have gym last period can just get dressed and go home, but we have to shower and try to look normal through the rest of the school day.

Then again, it only takes me about two minutes of standing under the hand dryer to make my hair look just as good as it usually does. Elana Logan is always late for third period, since she has this whole long process to go through after gym class every day. I feel a little bad for her, actually.

"I have to go to Mrs. J's room at lunch," I tell Keisha as we leave the locker room. "Will you come with me? She said she has to tell me something and I'm nervous about what it could be."

"Of course!" Keisha grins. "I'll see you then."

"Oh, man," Keisha groans when she gets to my locker after third period. "I'm so sore."

"From swimming?" We only swam four laps today — even *I* don't feel that terrible.

"No, not swimming. With play-offs coming up, we had practice all weekend. I was running like crazy." She shakes her left leg, loosening up her muscles. "I wasn't getting any passes, so I had to run after the ball if I wanted any action. Coach is making her decisions about our starters for play-offs, and I really want to be on that list."

"You will be!" I say confidently as we head down the hall. Keisha is the star of the team.

Keisha shakes her head. "This weekend, I felt pretty useless out there. It's almost like Stacey and Dahlia were keeping the ball away from me on purpose." She sighs. "I don't know what's going on."

I'm not all that surprised. Stacey seems to only look out for herself. If she's threatened by Keisha's soccer skills, she probably wanted to keep the ball away from her. "I'm sure you did a lot better than you think."

Keisha suddenly gets quiet and checks to see that no one is nearby, then says, "Jenna, I overheard them talking about 'Juicy Gossip' in the locker room on Friday."

"You did? What did they say?"

"Stacey's trying to find out who's writing it — she said she hates that someone knows so much about her and her friends. She said she has a hunch about who Little Miss Mango is."

"Do you think she knows it's me?" I start to get nervous and absentmindedly pick at my fingernails.

We're right outside Mrs. Jensen's classroom now, but Keisha pauses before opening the door. "No, I don't," she says. "I heard Jasmine Chen say that she knew for a fact that you're not Little Miss Mango."

"Why would she say that?"

Keisha looks really uncomfortable. "She said you just don't seem like the kind of person who would write 'Juicy Gossip.'" Keisha stops, but I know there's more.

"What else did she say, Keish? You're not telling me something."

"She was just being awful, Jenna." Keisha

moves to open Mrs. Jensen's classroom door, but I stop her. "You don't want to know."

"I do."

"She said that you're too clueless to know that much. She said it would take someone cool to write 'Juicy Gossip.'"

I can't decide if I'm angry or flattered. So Stacey, Jasmine, and Dahlia think I'm clueless and uncool? "Well," I say, "they're wrong, aren't they?"

"Jenna, are you okay?"

"Yeah." I pull open Mrs. J's classroom door. "Fine. In fact, I'm better than fine . . . because now, I don't even feel bad about writing 'Juicy Gossip.'"

Mrs. J greets us with a wave. "Hello, Jenna. Hello, Keisha. I have some good news."

"Really?" I don't know how good news is even possible right now. The newspaper is clearly getting cut, and the Seventh Grade Snobs think I'm completely lame.

"It seems you may have successfully turned the *Washington News* around. Last week, every copy was taken. Mrs. Liu has given us the go-ahead to publish it for a few more weeks and see how things go. We've even gotten a few calls from some parents who own local businesses. They want to put advertisements in the paper, which will help us bring in enough money to pay for the printing costs." Mrs. Jensen smiles. "Congratulations, Jenna."

Keisha slaps me on the back. "That's great news, Jenna!"

"Great," I echo. But I can't help feeling a little hollow. The only reason the paper is a success is that I'm printing trivial gossip about people. It's not because I include smart stories about important issues. Or interesting profile pieces on fascinating people at the school. Or even good movie reviews. It's only being read for "Juicy Gossip."

But I guess the newspaper's popularity had to start somewhere, or there would be no paper at all.

"Thanks a lot, Mrs. Jensen." I walk toward the door. "I'll see you after school — I have a paper to write!"

Keisha follows me into the hall. "So are you going to print another piece on the funding cuts this week? Do you need any help? Have you thought about who else is going to write articles? So many people are interested in being writers now. . . ." She keeps asking questions while I zone out.

What Mrs. J just told me is starting to sink in. I

may have saved the paper! I'm so distracted that I don't notice someone calling my name from near the center stairs. "Earth to Jenna." Keisha waves her hand in front of my face. "He's talking to you."

I turn, expecting to see Samir or Chris or another one of the newspaper's writers, but it's Peter. "Hey, Jenna. Hi," he says to Keisha.

Keisha is staring at Peter, and asks me — a little too loudly — "Who is that guy?"

"Hi, Peter," I say in response. "How's it going?"

"You know." He shrugs. "I'm on my way to math class — running a little late today. It happens."

"Well, have fun in math." I realize I have nothing to say. It's strange to see Peter in school, since I've only talked to him at the mall. "Are you working this week?"

Before Peter can answer, Stacey Smith's voice rings out from the end of the hall. "Jenna!" Keisha tenses up next to me. "Hey, Keisha. Hi, Peter."

Stacey knows Peter? I never would have expected that. I guess she's popular because she knows just about everyone. Peter holds out his hand to give Stacey a high five, and my stomach clenches up. They don't just know each other, they're *friends*.

"I'd better get to math. Mrs. Dahl is going to freak at me for being this late." Peter trots off down the hall, and Stacey, Keisha, and I all watch him go. Stacey sighs a little. "He's *cute*, isn't he?" She giggles. "Peter's in my gym class, and we made a great volleyball team!"

I just nod, since my throat is all tight. What am I supposed to say, anyway?

"So, girls." Stacey turns back to me and Keisha. "I was wondering if you wanted to come to Jasmine's birthday party this weekend? It's going to be superfun."

"Are you serious?" Keisha blurts out. "Us?"

Stacey shrugs. "Why not?"

I want to say no, since I know I'll feel completely out of place. But it might be kind of fun. And what better place to get more scoop for "Juicy Gossip" than at a Seventh Grade Snob's party? "Sure," I say quietly, nodding. "We'd love to."

Keisha's mouth hangs open. Stacey grins, then says, "Great! See you, girls." She heads off toward the cafeteria while Keisha and I stand in the middle of the hall, quietly staring after her.

"Why did you say we'll go?" Keisha snaps as soon as Stacey is out of earshot. "She only invited us because they want to find out who's writing 'Juicy Gossip' and think that if they get to be friends with you, you'll tell them. You know that, don't you?"

"Maybe," I admit. "But maybe not. Stacey invited me to sit with her at lunch last week. Maybe she wants to be friends because she actually likes me."

"Jenna, that's ridiculous." Usually Keisha's honesty is refreshing. Today, it's just making me feel bad. "Stacey's just being nice to us — well, *you*, really — because she wants something."

Ouch.

"But it's the perfect place for me to get more scoop for 'Juicy Gossip.'" I make my way toward the library, where I'm planning to spend the rest of lunch. Keisha follows, so I know she's not *really* mad at me. If she was, she'd go to the cafeteria to eat lunch with some of the other soccer girls. "You don't have to come to the party, you know."

"I know," she says.

"But I really want you to." I'm serious. I would feel so awkward showing up to the party alone, since I don't really know anyone. But more than anything, Keisha just makes everything more fun. "It won't be the same if you're not there."

"That's true." She gives me a tiny smile. "And I guess it will interesting, at least. Do you think Michael Hollings will be there? And speaking of guys, who was that Peter guy? Why haven't I heard of him?"

"Oh, no," I groan, ignoring her question about Peter. "Do you really think Michael will be at Jasmine's party?"

"Probably," Keisha says. "Still want to go?"

"Yes," I declare. "Absolutely." I try to sound confident, but I'm scared out of my mind. Me, Jenna Sampson, at a Seventh Grade Snob's party?

What have I gotten myself into?

CHAPTER ELEVEN

All week, I'm focused on Jasmine's party.

On Tuesday night, I have to work at Juice It, and realize that maybe I should spend one of my breaks shopping for something to wear on Saturday. I have some money saved from my birthday this summer. Keisha thinks it's hilarious that I have to actually shop at the mall, and spends most of lunch that day teasing me. That totally doesn't help.

As I stand behind the Juice It counter, chopping up pineapple, I study all the girls that walk by the booth in hopes of finding some sort of divine inspiration for what kind of outfit I can put together. I tell Junior about my dilemma, and he's full of suggestions. Of course.

"Ooh, how about something like that?" he offers, pointing to a sixty-year-old woman in a muumuu. It has flowers and bees all over it, and she's wearing a scarf around her head. "You'd make a real statement, Jenna."

"Cute," I say. "That's very cute, Junior. I need real help — can we be serious about this?"

"You could just wear your hat," he suggests, totally unhelpfully. "Actually, your pineapple hat would look great with that woman's dress!" He's giggling, and starts sort of hopping around the booth, all proud of himself for his ridiculous suggestions.

"What about something like that?" I ask him, nodding toward an older teenage girl wearing leather pants and a vintage-style T-shirt. "Could I get away with it?"

Junior steps back and holds a pineapple circle up to his eye. He looks at me through the little hole where the pineapple core used to be and says, "Nope. My fashion lens tells me that you would look very strange in that outfit."

"Your fashion lens?"

He places the pineapple slice down on the counter away from the rest of the fruit. (My dad is super-crazy about cleanliness, so if we ever touch anything without gloves it's considered "bad fruit" and it has to be tossed afterward.) "This pineapple is my fashion muse."

"How do you even know the word *muse*?" I ask. "You're nine."

"I'm very smart," Junior says, tapping his head and crossing his eyes.

"What about that?" I point to a girl wearing a skirt and a short sweater layered over a T-shirt.

"Jenna, you wear jeans every day. You'll look like a poser if you show up in a skirt."

"Poser? Junior, who have you been listening to? Where do you get these words?"

"Ooh, ooh." Junior perks up. "Look at those girls — that could be your style."

I look up and see Stacey Smith, Dahlia Levine, and Elana Logan walking through the food court. Just my luck. "That's Stacey Smith and her BFFs of the week," I tell Junior. "She's the most popular girl in seventh grade. She'll be at the party."

"Well, there you go," Junior says, knocking his pineapple hat into mine. "That's the look you need."

Yeah, easier said than done.

My dad turns on the CD player in our booth, and "The Lion Sleeps Tonight" blasts out of the speakers. I duck into the storeroom to avoid the stares of everyone in the food court, especially Stacey. When I peek out of the tiny storeroom window, I can see that my dad has started pounding on the counter in time to the music, using carrots as drumsticks. Junior is holding two pineapples up on the front counter, pretending they're dancing together.

Why me?

As the song ends, I spot Peter stepping out of the Moo La La booth across the food court. It looks like he's coming toward Juice It.

Luckily, the Seventh Grade Snobs just left, so I'm safe returning to my post. Weirdly, I'm suddenly sort of nervous about talking to Peter!

I approach the counter just in time to prevent my dad from taking Peter's order. Obviously, Peter is well aware of my embarrassing family since he can see us from his shop, but still. I'd prefer he not know just how completely crazy my dad is. "Hey, Peter."

"Ma'am, I'd like to try a smoothie," he says, smiling goofily at me. "I just love fruit, and would love to try one of your fine creations."

"Can I suggest a Blueberry Morning smoothie?" I act very professional, as though he's a real customer. My dad looks on, impressed. "It has honey, yogurt, and fine, ripe blueberries, rich in antioxidants."

"That sounds fantastic," Peter agrees, grinning.

My dad chimes in, "And don't forget, Jenna, that the Blueberry Morning smoothie also has a touch of our special Juice It potion: friendship and love to make your heart feel happy." My dad makes this little heart shape with his hands on his chest, and sort of bows to Peter.

Gulp. My dad just said "love" and *bowed* to Peter.

"Thanks, Dad," I say, trying to hide behind my hat. Can my life get any worse?

I step back behind the counter and make Peter's smoothie. When I pull off my gloves to ring it up, my hands are sort of shaky, and I accidentally knock his smoothie onto the floor.

My life is now much worse.

Peter laughs a little, which helps, but also doesn't. I know he's trying to make me feel better about my klutzy move, but he must think I'm a total spaz. Add my dad into the equation, and I look like the biggest oddball in the world.

"Thanks," Peter says when I hand him a new smoothie a few minutes later. "To be honest, this one looks even better than the first, so I'm kind of glad the first smoothie spilled." He grins again, making me feel a little less foolish.

"It's our treat," my dad says from behind me as Peter pulls out his money.

"Even better," Peter says, taking a slurp of his smoothie. "Thanks! This is delicious. See you, Jenna."

As Peter walks away, my dad starts asking all these questions about how I know him. I answer, trying to sound as casual as possible, then ask if I can take a break. Dad agrees, and hands me a little envelope with some cash in it.

"What's this for?" I ask.

"Liz told me I was supposed to give that to you on your break tonight. Something about clothes for a party this weekend?"

"Hey, thanks, Dad." I never buy clothes, so I'm sure Liz was pretty excited when I told her I needed to buy something.

I pull off my hat and smock and head out of the booth. As I get near the center courtyard, I hear someone call my name from inside The Edge. Stacey Smith is standing near the front of the store, holding several shirts in her hand. She waves, and I head over.

"Hi, Stacey," I say, looking nervously around at the clothes in the store. There's so much to pick from, and I don't even know where to start. It doesn't help that Stacey is with Dahlia and Elana. The last thing I need is Elana Logan, Fashion Queen of Seventh Grade, watching me try to buy an outfit. Talk about intimidating!

"Jenna!" Stacey says cheerfully. "What are you doing here?"

I can't tell her about Juice It, so I have no choice but to tell her I'm here looking for an outfit for the party. "I need something to wear on Saturday," I say awkwardly. "And I was looking for a gift for Jasmine. . . ."

"Ooh!" Stacey claps gleefully. "I can totally help you find something that would look great on you!" She looks me over carefully. "You usually have pretty cute jeans, actually. The most important thing is a more flattering shirt."

I lift my eyebrows. How is it so easy for her to identify my fashion challenges? I must look even worse than I thought. "Okay," I say quietly. "I like that one?" I point uncertainly to a purple T-shirt in her hand.

Stacey shakes her head and says, "That's what *I'm* wearing. Here, try this." She hands me a soft green shirt with a swirly pattern around the bottom. It feels really nice, and looks like it might be

104

okay-looking, too. "Go try it on," she demands, pointing toward the back of the store.

While I'm in the fitting room, I can hear Stacey and Elana talking. Elana sounds upset, and I hear her say something about her wrap skirt and "Juicy Gossip."

"Don't get so upset about it!" Stacey snaps. "It's just a dumb gossip column, Elana."

"So I guess that also means you didn't say your friends are boring?" Elana shoots back. Stacey says something that I can't hear, but it's clear that there are tensions within the Seventh Grade Snobs — and it seems like "Juicy Gossip" is to blame. But after what Keisha told me yesterday about them thinking I'm too uncool to be writing "Juicy Gossip," I have a hard time feeling guilty. Everything I printed was true. Maybe they just need to be a little more discreet about their gossiping?

When I step out of the fitting room, Stacey, Elana, and Dahlia are all trying on bracelets from a rack at the back of the store. I walk up and notice this really nice greenish one. Stacey sees me looking at it and says, "Jasmine would really like that." I realize she's trying to help me pick a gift for the party, which is actually helpful. Stacey's bossy, but also sort of nice. "Ohhh, Jenna," she goes on, looking at me in the shirt. "That's cute."

Elana nods slightly, which is enough for me. Done and done. I bring the shirt to the counter, and grab the green bracelet, too. I thank Stacey for her help, then make some excuse about my mom waiting for me in the car so I can get out of there. Once I'm sure they're not behind me, I scoot back to Juice It and slip into the back room to put my apron and hat on.

Keisha is sitting on the little stool in the back, slurping a smoothie. I jump a little. "Hey!" I say, surprised and happy to see her.

"I missed your break, didn't I?" Keisha says, looking disappointed. "I wanted to surprise you. . . . I came to help you shop!" She looks at the bag in my hand, then up at me. "Did you buy something by yourself? Oh, no, Jenna!"

I have to tell Keisha that Stacey helped me buy something for the party. However I say it, it's going to sound bad.

"I ran into Stacey, Elana, and Dahlia," I say. "It was a complete coincidence, but they helped me buy something — do you want to see?" I'm trying to be casual, but I know what Keisha is going to think.

"That's great, Jenna," Keisha says, sucking up

the last of her drink. "You're all set for the party. It doesn't seem like you need me at all, then."

"Keish, that's not true!" I say. "We should get you something for the party, too."

"I don't think we need to do that." Keisha stands up and walks out of the storeroom. "Later, Jenna. Good luck with 'Juicy Gossip' this week."

I shove my pineapple back onto my head and wander out to the smoothie station, wondering what I'm going to do to get my best friend's trust back.

CHAPTER TWELVE

JUICY GOSSIP
By Little Miss Mango

Rumors have to start somewhere — and what could be more fun than spreading the truth?

★ Little Miss Mango overheard a certain group of popular seventh grade girls talking about the Fall Carnival . . . and their secret plan to sabotage the dunk tank. Watch out!

★ Could our girls' soccer captain be guilty of prank-texting the school prankster? Someone was sending anonymous fake text messages to the seventh grade class clown to confess her crush . . . or were those messages real? Do soccer girl + prankster = ❤?

★ The blond cutie from last week's edition is still after Washington's third baseman . . . but it seems like Mr. Baseball may have lost interest. Stay tuned.

★ A female gem's birthday party is still on for this weekend. Who made the list? According to our sources, *not* everyone you'd expect was invited. That's not the way to hold on to your friends, birthday girl. . . .

"It looks like Little Miss Mango is spying again," Stacey's voice singsongs behind me. I'm at my locker after third period on Thursday, flipping through this week's edition of "Juicy Gossip." Keisha, who's waiting to go to Mrs. J's room with me for lunch, rolls her eyes.

Keisha and I haven't really talked more about my shopping trip at the mall earlier this week, but things still aren't totally back to normal between us. It sounds like Stacey is still on her mission to make Keisha look bad on the soccer field, and I think Keisha is upset that Stacey is being so nice to me.

Stacey leans against her locker and unfolds a copy of the paper. "She wrote about my friends again. Our friends." She looks at me meaningfully.

"Our friends?" I say. "What do you mean?"

"Jasmine was in 'Juicy Gossip' again this week. So was I. It was about all our friends."

Since when am I one of Stacey's friends? "Yeah," I say. "It's pretty crazy stuff."

"So we're still on for this weekend, right?" Stacey looks from me to Keisha. "You both made the list for the party."

I turn to Keisha, but she just stares back at me with no expression at all. "Of course we're still on," I say. "Wouldn't miss it."

I hear Keisha grunt a little bit. She seems so unlike herself lately. I don't understand why she's being so weird about Jasmine's party. I'm sure Stacey will realize how cool Keisha is when they hang out off the field. And it could even be my big chance with Michael.

"Well, I'm really excited for you to be there," Stacey says. "Jenna, I think you'll have a great time." She pauses and looks at Keisha with one eyebrow raised. "You too, Keisha. See you later, girls!"

When she's gone, Keisha turns to me and says, "She's so awful!"

"What do you mean?" I ask, slamming my locker shut. "She said she's excited for us to be there. She's being nice."

"You're totally getting sucked into her web!"

Keisha declares. "Since when do you fall for this stuff?"

"I'm not falling for anything!"

Keisha snorts, then changes the subject. "I have to go talk to Coach during lunch."

"Why?" I ask, walking with her toward Mrs. J's room. The paper has gotten so popular that I have to spend as much time there as I can, getting things ready for the next edition. "Don't you have practice after school?"

"Yeah," Keisha says quietly. "But I'm still not getting any passes on the field. I really think Stacey and Dahlia are keeping the ball from me on purpose. I want to talk to Coach and make sure she's not going to keep me out of the play-offs."

"Keish, that's terrible," I say, stopping in the middle of the hall. "Do you want me to talk to Stacey and find out what's going on? Maybe I can help."

"No!" Keisha turns to me, suddenly angry. "I don't want you to do anything. I think you've helped enough." Then she turns and jogs down the center stairs, before I have a chance to say anything.

On Saturday afternoon when I get home from the mall, I try to call Keisha. It goes right to voice mail.

Almost every weekend, one of her sisters is constantly on the phone. They both know my number, so they ignore me when the caller ID flashes that it's me on the other line.

Eager to figure out the plan for the party tonight, I turn on the computer in the kitchen. Keisha's logged into IM.

Editor Girl: Keish?
★ ★ ★ ★ ★

Editor Girl: HELLOOOOOO!?
Keish: Hey.
Editor Girl: What r u doing?
Keish: Reading.
Editor Girl: Cool. What time should my dad & I pick u up?
★ ★ ★ ★ ★

Editor Girl: Hello?
Keish: I can't go.
Editor Girl: WHAT??!!
Keish: Sorry.
Editor Girl: I can't go alone!
Keish: U will be fine. They luv u.
Editor Girl: I don't want to go w/o u.
Keish: U will have more fun if I'm not there.
Editor Girl: K – that's stupid.

112

★ ★ ★ ★ ★

Editor Girl: U know I have to get more scoop.
I have 2 go.
Keish: I know, J.
Editor Girl: R u mad?
Keish: Gotta go. Claudia needs the computer.

She logs out, and her screen name turns into a gray shadow.

I can't figure out what's going on, but I feel sick. I'm sort of stuck. I want to go to the party to get more scoop for the paper so people will keep reading it, but I don't want to ruin things forever with my best friend. But it's up to me to get the word out about the budget cuts, and this is my best shot. I may never have a chance to hang out with Stacey and her friends again.

Maybe if I become better friends with them, they'll be nicer to Keisha. It can't hurt to try. Plus, I'm definitely excited about seeing what Michael is like beyond the walls of Madame Fishman's classroom.

I decide to go to the party alone. What's the worst that could happen?

"Jen-*nah*!" The way Stacey says my name makes it sound like two words. "Jasmine, Jenna's here!" I'm standing outside the door at Jasmine's house. When Stacey announces my arrival, it makes me feel like a celebrity or something. It's like they've been waiting just for me.

Everyone except Stacey and Jasmine is already in the basement. Stacey skips into Jasmine's kitchen, and I follow a little less enthusiastically. "Hi, Jasmine," I say, feeling like my tongue is sort of big and clumsy. "Thanks for inviting me."

I hand Jasmine my gift — the green bracelet I bought while I was shopping with Stacey — and she tosses the bag on her kitchen island.

"Thanks." Jasmine smiles, pouring a big bag of chips into a bowl. "I'm glad you could come!"

I seriously feel like I just ate a whole thing of peanut butter. It's like my tongue is stuck to the roof of my mouth.

Stacey is sucking on a cherry lollipop, studying me carefully. "What did you do today, Jenna?" she asks, as though she knows the answer.

They've lured me here to trap me. They know all about how I can hear everything while I'm working at the juice bar, and they know that I'm the one writing "Juicy Gossip," and they're going to confront me tonight.

I definitely should not have come.

"Are you okay?" Stacey pulls the lollipop out of her mouth and stares.

"Mmm-hmm," I murmur. My face is red and I'm starting to sweat.

Jasmine pops a chip into her mouth. "So, Jenna." She frowns. "What *did* you do today? Stacey asked you. . . ."

I'm scared. I can't think of an escape route, and my dad already drove off, so I don't have a ride home until ten o'clock. I'm totally cornered. My mouth is still refusing to talk.

Jasmine stares at me. "Okaaay," she says finally. "I'm going downstairs."

"Keisha couldn't come?" Stacey asks. I just shake my head. "Hmm, I'm surprised." Then she perks up. "Oh, well, come on. Let's go hang out with everyone in the basement. Jasmine just got Dance Dance Revolution — have you played?"

I can feel the peanut butter melting in my mouth. "No," I say quietly. "My parents' idea of new technology is a karaoke machine."

Stacey laughs. "That's funny." She links her arm through mine as we walk down the stairs. "You're funny, Jenna."

"Thanks." I can see why Stacey is so popular. She has this way of making me feel like a superstar when I'm with her. I'm totally getting lured into her trap.

At the bottom of the stairs, there's a big fridge stocked with soda and Stacey grabs Cokes for both of us. I don't really like Coke, but I take it, anyway. We walk past an exercise bike and a treadmill, and into this little den area in Jasmine's basement. Most people are watching Jeremy Rosenberg and Jasmine start a round of Dance Dance Revolution on Wii. Jeremy has slipped his shoes off to play, and his feet smell so bad that I'm pretty sure I can see a little cloud of odor wafting up from his brown socks. Ew.

Stacey flops down on a big red beanbag chair and gestures for me to sit next to her. A few people look at us as we walk in, but mostly everyone is engrossed in what's happening on the Wii. It gives me a few minutes to sit there and take it all in.

There's a big basketball arcade game in one corner of the den. Michael Hollings and Robbie Prinzo are shooting hoops and pushing each other around. Jasmine put the chips on a countertop that runs along one wall of the room, and Dahlia Levine is sitting next to the bowl, watching Michael's every move. A few of the other Seventh Grade Snobs — Elana, Katherine, and Brittany — are texting someone on Elana's phone while they watch Jeremy dance. I wonder if Stacey and Jasmine decided to invite them after Little Miss Mango told everyone about the party?

I'm just sitting there, minding my own business, when suddenly Michael is sitting next to me. He doesn't say anything, so I pretend not to notice him, since Dahlia is giving me an evil look from the other side of the room.

Stacey leans forward in her beanbag chair. "It's sort of creepy when you just sit there, Michael." She laughs. "Are you going to say anything?" She looks at me and says, jokingly, "Michael thinks he's this silent, mysterious guy. He must think it makes him seem really cute or something."

Michael gives her the annoyed look that's usually reserved for me. Then he rolls his eyes. "*Hey*, Stacey. Hi, Jenna."

"That's better," Stacey says.

"Hi," I say at the same time. I don't think Michael hears me.

He continues to sit there, leaving me paralyzed. I pretend to stare at the TV, but really I'm sort of watching Michael out of the corner of my eye. I can't really think about anything except that he's sitting this close to me *voluntarily*. I feel guilty admitting it to myself, but it was totally worth coming to the party without Keisha for this moment.

After a few minutes, it's Michael's turn on the Wii. He asks if I want to play Guitar Hero with him, but I just sort of shake my head no. I've never played, so it would be the best way to look like a total freak in front of everyone. I'm relieved when they turn off the Wii and turn on *High School Musical*. The guys all groan, but Stacey announces that it's Jasmine's birthday and she gets to watch whatever she wants.

Everyone chats and sings along through most of the movie, and I talk to Brittany for a while. She and I went to elementary school together, and she's always been pretty nice. But she keeps pulling out her phone to text, so I get up to grab a few chips. Stacey links her arm in mine while she watches Jeremy shoot hoops, then leads me back to the beanbags to watch the movie next to her.

All in all, the party is actually sort of boring. I don't talk to that many people, since almost everyone stays in little pods of two or three people, and I don't really know where I fit in. Stacey keeps turning away from me to talk to girls on her other side, and I'm left alone a lot.

If it hadn't been for the few magical Michael moments, I'd say that this night made me feel even more out of it than before. Even my Michael interaction was weird, I had to admit.

Sometimes he's mean, sometimes he's nice, but he only really notices me when I'm hanging out with the popular girls. It makes me a little sick to think about. I can't help wondering why I'm okay with that.

Brittany and Katherine come over to show me a video they downloaded onto Brittany's phone from YouTube, when all of a sudden I hear Stacey say, "Keisha is totally snooping in on our conversations." She's talking to Dahlia, and I don't think they know that I'm listening to them. Or if they do, they don't care.

"That's so like her," Dahlia says.

Stacey surprises me by saying, "She's nice and all, but you just can't trust her."

Keisha? She's the most trustworthy person on earth. I could tell her anything, and she would keep it a secret forever if I asked her to.

I sit there quietly, eager to hear more of the conversation. I've gotten to be an expert at eavesdropping, which is not something I'm proud of. Katherine Szuchman and I have *way* too much in common — and Katherine was so busy text messaging gossip to other people tonight that she dropped her cell phone in the toilet. Do I really want to have anything in common with someone like that? Yuck.

Dahlia crunches on a chip. The room suddenly gets very loud, and I have a hard time hearing her and Stacey. But it seems to get deathly silent again when Dahlia says, "I think Keisha *must* be Little Miss Mango."

WHAT?! It takes every muscle in my neck to keep my head from spinning around to stare at them in disbelief.

Then Stacey says, "I know. She must be listening to our conversations in the locker room after soccer practice and then printing them in 'Juicy Gossip.'" Her voice lowers to a whisper. "She *is* Jenna's best friend, after all. And we *know* she writes for the newspaper. She's the only person that can hear all our gossip and would want to spread it around."

Dahlia must be nodding, because she doesn't say anything else. My mind won't stop spinning. Even when my dad comes to pick me up later, I can't stop thinking about what I overheard at the party. They think Keisha is writing "Juicy Gossip"?

I went to Jasmine's party to get more scoop for "Juicy Gossip" — but instead, I just got a stomachache. My best friend is in trouble with the Seventh Grade Snobs, and it's all my fault.

CHAPTER THIRTEEN

"Mr. Hankel just told me the Fall Carnival will probably be canceled." Stacey plunks down in her seat at the lunch table on Monday with a big frown on her face. "I can't believe it."

Elana Logan runs her hand through her silky red hair and asks, "Why would they cancel the Fall Carnival? It's so much fun!"

Stacey nods. "I know! But I guess it costs a lot more than the school can afford. It's supposed to be a fund-raiser, but we end up losing a bunch of money every year."

I sit there silently, just like the first time I sat with Stacey and her friends during lunch. It's the Monday after Jasmine's birthday party, and Stacey invited me to join her again in the "caf."

I was hoping to have lunch with Keisha, since

she seemed so bitter about the party this week-end. I haven't even told her about the Seventh Grade Snobs thinking she's Little Miss Mango yet! But she said she had something else to do during lunch.

Now that I'm sitting at Stacey's table, I'm regretting not spending lunch on the next issue of the newspaper. It seems like people still don't know a lot about the budget cuts, even though we've had huge stories on the front cover of the paper for the last two weeks. I guess people are only reading "Juicy Gossip." I need to figure out a way to shake things up soon, or I'm the editor of a gossip column — and that's about it.

I take a bite of my salami sandwich and glance around the cafeteria. A familiar head of black curls catches my eye. It's Keisha, sitting with some girls from her third period civics class! She ditched me to sit with other people? I feel one hundred percent awful. She glances at me and we lock eyes — but then she turns away and laughs at something. My stomach clenches.

"You have to find a way to out her," Dahlia is whispering, once I start paying attention to the conversation at the Seventh Grade Snobs' table again.

"I will," Stacey says. "She can't eavesdrop like that and get away with it."

Stacey and Dahlia are talking about Keisha and "Juicy Gossip" again! I turn my head, trying to listen in. But when Stacey notices me paying attention, she makes a shushing sound to Dahlia. "So, Jenna," she says, changing the subject. "Did you have fun at the party this weekend? Michael seemed pretty excited to see you there."

I shrug, blushing. Stacey oohs, but quickly enough the conversation turns away from me and on to some sort of shoe discussion. I'm relieved.

But I'm also desperate to know how Stacey is planning to find out if Keisha is Little Miss Mango. Especially since it's *me* they should be going after . . . not my best friend.

"Grab those lemons for me, will you, Jen?" Liz gestures with an armful of bananas. I stuff two lemons between a few bananas that are wedged in her arms. Since it's Monday night, the mall is pretty slow, so my dad asked us to stock the smoothie station. I sort of get the impression that we're just moving fruit around to keep busy.

As soon as Liz comes back to the smoothie station with a stack of lids, I blurt out, "Liz, I need help."

She rubs my shoulder. "Did you forget how to juice oranges? Need me to give you a little tutorial?"

"I don't need help with the fruit." I'm not a crying sort of person. But all of a sudden, I just want to sob. Everything is going so wrong, and I don't know how to fix it. "I guess I just need some advice."

"You've come to the right person," she says, and plunks down on a stool. "I'm a mom, so advice is what I do best."

"I know, Liz." She is such a goof. "So I had this big plan, and it was going really well, and then it started falling apart, and now Keisha sort of hates me, and I don't know what to do about it."

"Whoa." Liz starts cracking up. It's not really funny that she's laughing at my misery, but since it's Liz, I don't mind. "Slow down, babe."

"Sorry." I start from the beginning and tell her about "Juicy Gossip." "I just wanted to save the paper. And if people started reading the paper, I thought they'd learn about the budget cuts and band together to try to save our school activities."

"So people are reading the newspaper now? That sounds like a good thing."

"Yeah, but they're only reading 'Juicy Gossip.' They're not reading the other stories. I saved the newspaper, but I haven't done anything to keep the other activities from being cut."

"You're trying, sweetie." Liz looks so hopeful. "That's something."

"And Keisha's mad at me, which doesn't help."

Liz pauses, before saying, "Why is Keisha mad at you? That's probably the most important thing to figure out."

"I guess it's because she doesn't really like my gossip column."

Liz looks at me meaningfully. "Does she dislike the gossip column, or is it something deeper than that?" Liz is very into feelings. She studied psychology in college and is pretty obsessed. It's usually a little too sentimental for my taste, but I kind of get what she's saying this time.

"You mean, like, she doesn't like the way 'Juicy Gossip' is affecting our friendship?" Whoa, I sound deep. "I guess maybe she doesn't like that Stacey Smith and Jasmine Chen and the Seventh Grade Snobs are suddenly paying attention to me."

Liz laughs. "*Who* are the 'Seventh Grade Snobs'? And why do they call themselves that? What a terrible name!"

"They don't call themselves that. It's my secret name for them."

Liz chuckles again. "You'd better be careful. That's not a nice thing to call them. But you know that."

"Yeah, I do. But they *can* be snobby, and they're not very nice to Keisha at soccer, either."

"Didn't you go to a birthday party for Jasmine this weekend?"

"Yeah, but mainly to get scoop for 'Juicy Gossip.' I'm not actually friends with any of them," I confess. "That makes me sound really terrible, doesn't it?"

Liz studies me carefully. "Have you thought that maybe Keisha doesn't like this new Jenna? A Jenna who goes to parties with people she doesn't like just to publish what they're saying in her school newspaper?"

"Liz, it's not like that."

"But Keisha may see it that way. She may see it as cuddling up with the enemy, if those girls are treating her badly at soccer."

She's right. Keisha is probably sick of the fact that I've been all into the Seventh Grade Snobs. I guess it does seem like I'm willing to be friends with them even though they're freezing my best

126

friend out on the field. I guess I *have* been a little obsessed.

But the thing is, I've actually started to like Stacey. She's kind of nice, and has been really welcoming. Then again, she and her friends are being horrible to Keisha at soccer. But is it just because they think she's writing "Juicy Gossip"?

"Liz, the Seventh Grade Snobs think that Keisha is behind 'Juicy Gossip.' I heard them talking about it at Jasmine's party this weekend."

"That's not good," she says. "Sounds like you may have to tell everyone you're the mystery columnist."

"Little Miss Mango."

"Little Miss Mango? That's what you call yourself?" Liz laughs. "That's clever, Jenna."

"I thought so. But Liz, can I make things right for Keisha and help with the school funding cuts at the same time?" I stop to think for a second, and Liz rolls an orange around in circles on the counter. "I mean, if I could use the newspaper to help raise the money we need for the other activities, it would all be worth it. I'm sure Keisha would forgive me."

Liz sits quietly, thinking. "So if there's some

way you could use 'Juicy Gossip' as a good thing, rather than just a means of spreading gossip . . ."

"What if I could get everyone to go to the Fall Carnival? If everyone at school came and brought their families, we could actually raise a lot of money."

"How would you do that?"

I chew my fingernail. "If I could create a story about something really big and gossip-worthy happening at the Fall Carnival, then everyone would show up. I could make something up and print it in 'Juicy Gossip.'"

"It could work, Jenna," Liz says. "Or not. But it can't hurt to try. And I think we both know it's important that you fix things with Keisha. You need to figure out how to balance your role as Little Miss Mango with your role as a good friend."

I know that she's right. I've been pretty caught up in the world of the Seventh Grade Snobs lately. I guess I was so busy enjoying my newfound popularity that I forgot it's not what I was looking for.

Just then, a customer comes to the counter, and Liz pats me on the shoulder before going over to help her. I absentmindedly cut oranges and stuff them into the juicer.

The juicer is pretty loud, but when the whir of its motor quiets, I hear Stacey Smith's voice ringing through the food court. She's sitting at a nearby table saying — something about me.

I wipe my hands on a towel and stand quietly, trying to listen to their conversation. But they start whispering, and get up to leave before I can hear anything else.

Junior comes strolling into the booth with a bunch of empty trays that he'd collected from out in the food court. "I just saw your friend, Stacey, and all of her friends," he says. "They like to talk — a lot."

"What about?" I ask. "What were they saying?"

"The girl in the blue —"

I cut him off. "Jasmine?"

"Sure," he says, shrugging. "She was saying something about two people named Michael and Dahlia getting caught almost-kissing on the soccer field. I guess your principal, Mrs. Liu, found them!"

My stomach drops. "Are you sure?" That can't be true. It seemed like he wasn't at all into her at Jasmine's party!

"Positive," Junior says, tapping his pineapple hat. "Then they said something about someone named Little Miss Mango."

"What about Little Miss Mango?" I say, hoping Junior remembers the rest.

"The same girl said something like, 'We'll see what Little Miss Mango has to say about that — and then we'll know.' Then she snorted out this really icky laugh and that's when I got out of there. She sounded like a donkey, Jenna."

Then they'll know *what*?

I only know one thing for sure — thanks to Junior, Little Miss Mango just got a very juicy bit of gossip for this week's newspaper.

CHAPTER FOURTEEN

JUICY GOSSIP
By Little Miss Mango

★ Romance is in the air for two of Washington's lovebirds. The blond ponytailed cutie and her third-base-playing crush were caught by Mrs. Liu, almost-kissing on the soccer field. I guess this romance is on its way to detention!

★ We hear the girl gem's birthday party was a smashing success. The one mishap? Rumor has it that a tall brunette dropped her cell phone in the toilet during the party. It didn't break, so she continued to send text messages on it. Gross!

★ The Fall Carnival is right around the corner — or is it? This year's Carnival might be canceled. Too bad, because if at least five hundred people show up, I, Little Miss Mango, will reveal my identity at the Carnival. Are you going?

"Do you think I'm the person Little Miss Mango is talking about?" It's the middle of French class, and Michael has been reading "Juicy Gossip" under his desk whenever Madame Fishman isn't looking. "*I* play third base on Washington's baseball team."

I shrug. "I guess it must be you."

"But I wasn't caught almost-kissing Dahlia!" Madame Fishman looks at us with stern, bulgy eyes. Michael lowers his voice to a whisper. "I don't even like Dahlia. *Christian* does." His brownie-colored eyes look at me pitifully.

"Really?"

"*Oui,*" he whispers in French. "I like someone else."

"You do?"

"*Oui.*" The look he's giving me makes me realize he's talking about . . . me. My stomach lurches violently.

The moment is broken when someone across the room coughs, and Michael turns around to give them his signature rude look. When he does, I realize he gives *everyone* the evil look I originally thought was reserved especially for me. He turns back to me and rolls his eyes, and I'm suddenly super-aware that he really is — at his core — a jerk. He's not silent and mysterious. He's just sort of rude and judgmental and, well, mean.

And cuteness does not make up for rudeness. Even when it's Michael Hollings.

I want to hang out with people who will like me and be friendly to me, whether or not I'm popular or unpopular or cool or uncool. The reason I get along with Keisha is that she likes me because I'm just Jenna.

"Well," I say to Michael. "Good luck with that. But you and Dahlia would have made a good couple." And then I turn back to my workbook, pretending to be engrossed in French.

"Jenna, the Seventh Grade Snobs think I'm Little Miss Mango. What did you tell them?" Keisha storms up to me after third period on Tuesday — the day the new issue of "Juicy Gossip" was printed — waving around a copy of the *Washington News*. "Stacey cornered me in third period and said she knows it's me."

"Whoa," I say, "calm down." This probably sounds really irritating, and I'm sure of it as soon as it comes out of my mouth.

"Calm down?" Keisha is literally fuming. I think

she might have smoke coming out of her ears. "This is all your fault, Jenna. You *know* I'm not Little Miss Mango! This is the reason they've all been shutting me out on the field. They think *I'm* the one who's printing all this gossip about them." She stares at me with one of her fiercest looks ever. "You *have* to come clean."

"Keish, I'm sorry," I say, really, truly meaning it. "I didn't mean for this to happen. Listen, everything is all messed up and I'm trying to fix it." I put my hand on her arm, but she brushes it off. "I overheard Stacey and her friends talking about how they thought you were Little Miss Mango, and I wanted to tell you, but you've been avoiding me since the party. You haven't even let me talk to you long enough for me to tell you that. I swear, I'm going to fix it."

"How? Stacey and Dahlia have been going out of their way to make me look terrible on the field. We have one game left — today — and if I don't look a whole lot better out there, I'm not a starter for play-offs."

"I'll fix it, I promise. And I'm going to reveal my identity at the Fall Carnival next week. I'm trying to use the Carnival as a way to raise some money for the school and save our activities," I explain, tears springing to my eyes. "If enough people come to the Carnival, I'm pretty sure we can make enough money to save soccer, lacrosse, and maybe even debate. The Carnival could be a great fund-raiser — even Stacey said so."

"*Stacey* said so? That's why you're doing it? Do you really think people will come just to find out who's writing 'Juicy Gossip'?"

"Yup." I nod, chewing my fingernail. I hate when Keisha is mad at me. "I hope it works."

"So do I." She's clearly still fuming. "Why do Stacey and her friends think I'm the one writing your column?" she asks after a minute.

"I don't know," I say. "I overheard them saying that they thought you were eavesdropping on their conversations in the locker room after practice."

Keisha snorts. "Everyone hears their conversations in the locker room. It's one room, and they talk loud. It's like they *want* the rest of the team to hear them. Why wouldn't they suspect Jenny or Clara . . . or Stella, even?"

"I think it's because they know you're a writer for the newspaper. Keisha, I really didn't mean for this to happen. I didn't think you'd get in trouble because of my gossip column."

"But I did." Stacey and Dahlia are sauntering down the hall toward Stacey's locker, so we both go silent.

"Hey, girls," Stacey says. "Jenna, we figured out who your mystery writer is."

"I don't think you did."

"Don't be so sure of that," Dahlia says. "We planted a little test for you, Keisha. You failed."

Keisha furrows her brow. "What do you mean, a test?"

"I mean —" Dahlia smiles at Stacey, then looks back at Keisha. "— I was *not* caught almost kissing Michael on the soccer field. Michael and I are *friends*. We made that up, and Stacey talked about it in the locker room after practice on Monday. We knew that if it was printed in 'Juicy Gossip,' you'd be guilty." She holds out a copy of the paper. "And there it is."

"You caught me," Keisha deadpans. "I guess I'm Little Miss Mango."

"That's a lie, Keish." I shake my head at her. I turn to Stacey and Dahlia. "I know who Little Miss Mango is, and it's not Keisha."

"Unless you tell us who the real author of 'Juicy Gossip' is, we can't believe that," Stacey says bossily. "It seems like you're cornered, Keisha." Stacey grabs her lunch bag out of her locker, slams the door, and grabs Dahlia's arm. With a flip of her hair, she saunters back down the hall with her latest BFF in tow.

"I'll fix this, Keisha," I say, turning toward my best friend as soon as they're out of earshot. "You have to trust me."

Keisha is very quiet when she finally says, "How did *you* hear about Dahlia and Michael kissing on the soccer field?"

"Junior overheard them talking about it at the mall," I say, sighing. "They must have been talking about their scheme to catch you. But I guess he only heard the fake gossip." I smile sheepishly. "I guess their plan wasn't really so foolproof, since the real Little Miss Mango got the same piece of fake gossip."

Keisha looks at me without smiling. "But *I'm* the one being punished for Little Miss Mango's gossiping. Thanks, Jenna." She turns and storms down the hall.

I make my way toward Mrs. J's room alone. I have to figure out a way to get out of the mess I've put my best friend in — or she might not be my friend at all anymore.

CHAPTER FIFTEEN

Sometime between lunch and the end of the school day, I figure out how I'm going to fix things for Keisha. It's not her fault that the Seventh Grade Snobs are mad at her — let's face it, that's completely my problem — so it's totally up to me to make things right.

Immediately.

Today's soccer game is the last one of the regular season, and it's just the event I need to put my plan in place. But before I can do that, I have to convince my parents to give me the afternoon off work. I catch the city bus from school up to the mall, and make my way through the central courtyard toward Juice It.

As I pass The Edge, I hear someone call my name. My stomach gets all fluttery — it's Peter.

Now that I realize how much I'm *not* into Michael, I'm pretty sure I'm suffering from a major case of crushing on Peter. Today he's wearing a shirt that says: WORDS ARE MY WEAPONS. I love that.

"Hey, Peter." I smile at him, struggling to stay cool.

"Jenna," he says, waving at me. "How's it going?"

We walk together toward the food court. "You're working today?" I ask. I realize I don't know what else to talk to him about. I don't even know if he plays sports or anything. Washington is *way* too big. It's so weird that we're in the same grade and never see each other.

"Yeah," he says. "Hey, I've been meaning to ask you something, Jenna."

Heart fluttering, I keep my voice calm. Is he going to ask me to go to Fall Carnival with him? Or to the movies?

"You edit the newspaper, right?"

"Oh." My heart stops fluttering. I guess I don't have to worry about whether or not my dad will be painfully embarrassing if he has to drive me and Peter to the movies. "Right."

"So you must know who this Little Miss Mango person is."

"Yep," I say. Even Peter is obsessed with "Juicy Gossip"? Argh.

Peter turns to look at me. "I wish she would stop."

"Stop what?"

"Stop writing 'Juicy Gossip.' It's pretty terrible." He shakes his head.

"But it got people interested in the newspaper!" I protest. "It was the only way to get people to start reading it!" I sound really defensive, but I can't help it.

Peter chuckles a little. "Whoa, whoa — you're not the one to blame, Jenna. But I'm sure you have enough influence to make whoever's writing the column stop spreading all that horrible gossip."

My lip starts to quiver. I'm pretty close to tears again. What's *with* me this week? "Okay," I say lamely. "Thanks for the feedback. See you, Peter." Then I head off toward Juice It. I may have saved the newspaper, but I may have also lost some friends (and a potential crush) along the way.

By the time I get to Juice It, convince my parents to let me have the afternoon off, and head back to the soccer field, Keisha's game is almost half over. Washington is losing — by a lot — and it's uglier than I thought it would be. Chris Dotman is covering the game for the newspaper, so I sit with him for the rest of the first half.

With a few minutes left before halftime, Keisha starts hustling along the edge of the field, totally open. No one is paying any attention to her. She's running like mad, trying to get into scoring position. Stacey runs the ball all the way up the field herself and takes a shot. She misses, then pretends she didn't even see that Keisha was wide open on the other side of the goal.

The whistle blows — halftime. I see Keisha looking up at the stands, but I duck down. I don't want her to see me. If she saw me talking to Stacey, she'd be even angrier . . . and that's what I'm about to do. Stacey is my best hope for fixing everything — if I straighten things out with her, I know she can help clear things up with her other friends.

I stand under the bleachers, peeking out from between two benches. After a quick powwow with their coach, the team splits up to stretch. Stacey and Dahlia are chatting a few feet away from me. It's eerily similar to the position I often find myself in at the mall. I can hear everything they're saying, but they can't see me.

This time, though, I *want* Stacey to notice me. "Stacey," I whisper. She looks around, confused.

141

"Over here." I feel like a spy. And I imagine I look completely crazy, peeking out from under the bleachers.

"Jenna?" she asks, spotting me. "What are you doing under there?" She gives me a look and sort of rolls her eyes at Dahlia. I don't care what they think. She can roll her eyes until they pop out, for all I care. I just need to get things straightened out for Keisha.

"Come here," I whisper. Stacey sighs this deep, heavy sigh like I've asked her to commit a major crime, but saunters under the bleachers.

"This is really weird, Jenna." She shakes her head at me. "What's going on?"

"Listen," I start. "I have to tell you something, but I need you to hear me out before you snap to any judgments."

Stacey sniffs. "Whatever."

"I'm Little Miss Mango."

"What?" Stacey's eyes get wide. "That's impossible. You're too nice, Jenna — you really shouldn't cover for your friend."

"I'm not. I'm telling the truth. Will you keep listening?"

Stacey eyes me suspiciously, then nods.

I continue. "You know the new juice bar — Juice It — that opened at the mall a few weeks ago? Well, my parents own it, and I work there." I literally tell her everything in less than two minutes flat. She listens intently, and starts to smile. "So," I say finally, "I really am Little Miss Mango. But here's the part where I need your help."

"*You*," Stacey stresses the word, "need *my* help? After everything you've printed about me the last few weeks? I thought we were starting to be friends, but you were just using me to get information for your newspaper." Stacey genuinely looks upset.

"I wasn't using you!" I cry. "I thought *you* were just being friendly to *me* so you could find out who was writing 'Juicy Gossip'!" I figure it can't hurt to be honest. What do I have to lose, anyway?

Stacey looks hurt. "I wouldn't do that," she says firmly. "You might think I'm a snob or something, but I really thought we could be friends. I like you, Jenna. You make me laugh, and you're so comfortable just being yourself."

Isn't this a strange turn of events?

"Okay," I say, trying to hide my surprise. "Well then, as a friend, I need your help."

Stacey narrows her eyes at me. "What is it?"

"I want you to stop shutting Keisha out of the game. She didn't have anything to do with

'Juicy Gossip,' and shouldn't be tortured on the field."

"That's a good point," Stacey says, looking guilty. "Anyway, we need her help out there. She's our only hope to turn this game around."

I smile, happy to hear Stacey compliment Keisha like that. "Also, I need you to help me keep Little Miss Mango's identity under wraps until next week."

"Why would I do that?" she snaps.

"Because I'm hoping to reveal everything at the Fall Carnival. I think there will be enough curiosity about who's writing 'Juicy Gossip' that a ton of people will show up." Stacey looks intrigued. "I have a few ideas for how we can convince the school to let us have the Fall Carnival, and how we can raise a lot more money than ever before. But we need to make sure we can get people there."

"That's a decent plan, Jenna," Stacey says. "But if I have to help you with your plan, then I have an idea, too. . . ."

By the time the whistle blows to start the second half, Stacey and I have the skeleton of a plan outlined for the Fall Carnival, and we've agreed to meet up after school next week to talk more.

I stay for the second half of the game, cheering as loudly as possible. I jump to my feet when Keisha tips her third goal (with an assist by Stacey) into the net. Washington is up by two, my best friend is a star, and things are finally turning around.

CHAPTER SIXTEEN

"It's almost time!" Stacey announces to a huge crowd at the Fall Carnival. "Little Miss Mango will be revealed in mere moments!"

I sit shivering behind a large black tarp, wondering if this was all worth it. The water from the dunk tank looms cold and deep below, ready to swallow me up as soon as a ball hits the little blue target.

The tarp falls away, and everyone can see me sitting inside the dunk tank in my brother's shorts and a Juice It T-shirt. A LITTLE MISS MANGO sign hangs above my head.

"And now," Stacey announces, "step right up and take your shot at Jenna Sampson, editor of the esteemed *Washington News* and . . . our very own Little Miss Mango!"

Robbie Prinzo steps forward and hands Stacey a dollar. Stacey gives Robbie five balls, and he lines up to fire them at me. He throws, and a second later I'm swirling around in the water that had, only moments before, loomed cold and untouched below me.

"Aghhhh!" I yell. "It's coooold!"

Everyone laughs, and I climb back up on my perch to let someone else take their shot. Dahlia takes a turn, then Jasmine, Katherine Szuchman . . . pretty much everyone I wrote about in "Juicy Gossip" looks ecstatic about getting the chance to try to dunk me. Everyone else is just enjoying my misery.

Finally, Keisha steps up to the line and wiggles her finger at me. "I told you it was a bad idea," she says, then aims and throws her ball. I can tell she misfired on purpose. She does the same thing with her next three balls. When she only has one ball left in her hand, she shrugs her shoulders, smiles sweetly, and hits a perfect shot. Down I go, water rushing up my nose as I plunge to the bottom of the dunk tank.

"Thanks, Keish," I yell, climbing back up to sit on the platform again. "You're a real friend!" I laugh.

She smiles back at me. "*Now* we're even."

After the game last week, I followed Keisha all the way home, apologizing like crazy and explaining everything. It took a *lot* of sorrys, but I finally convinced her that I understood why she was mad and knew I had gone a little overboard with my plan.

It was Keisha's idea to have Stacey Smith take over as the new Little Miss Mango (with a new name, of course). Stacey is so excited to be the new Queen of Washington Gossip for the newspaper, and this way, I should be able to keep myself out of trouble!

"Okay, everyone," Stacey announces bossily. "Even Little Miss Mango deserves a break. A few more minutes, and then we'll let her dry off. Mrs. Liu will be next in the dunk tank! Get your dollars out!"

The cool October wind is blowing and it feels like icicles are forming on my wet shorts and T-shirt. But before I can escape the dunk tank, one more person comes forward to take his shots.

"*Bon jour,*" Michael yells to me as he exchanges a dollar for five balls. "*Pardonez moi,* Jenna!"

The first shot is a little off, but the second one hits the center of the target, and I'm sailing downward again. The splash shocks me. "*Merci,* Michael," I shout from the water. He smiles slightly, then gives me his classic Michael look. Some things never change.

When I'm finally released from the dunk tank, I'm pretty sure I've never been this cold in my life. My towel and dry clothes are all the way back in the locker room, and I don't know how I'm going to make it that far. Shivering, I climb down the ladder and hop off the last step, ready to make a run for it.

But when I turn around, I see a big, fuzzy beach towel right in front of me. "Need this?" Peter says. He's holding it up like a dunk tank hero or something. "You look cold."

"Thanks," I say, relieved that I'm blushing a little bit since it's helping my cheeks warm up.

"So you're Little Miss Mango, huh?" Peter looks disappointed. "I guess that's why you were so upset when I asked you about it."

"I guess." There's not much else to say.

"'Juicy Gossip' doesn't really seem like something you would write," Peter says. Okay, now I'm totally embarrassed.

"It usually *wouldn't* be something I would write," I explain. "But when the paper was at risk, I had to do whatever I could." I pause to dry my hair and wrap the towel around me. "My goal was to get people to start reading the paper again. I

149

really wanted people to pay attention to every-thing else we cover in the paper — like the budget cuts — but I sort of lost sight of the original plan." I shrug.

"I don't know about that," Peter says. "It seems like you got a pretty huge crowd to show up to the Fall Carnival. And I read in the paper — your paper — that we're using the Fall Carnival as a fund-raiser to help save Washington's activities?"

"You read the rest of the paper?" I ask as we climb the steps into school.

"Of course," Peter says, furrowing his brow. "Did you think I just read the gossip?"

I laugh. "Everyone else does."

Peter shakes his head. "I don't think that's true — I've seen a lot of people reading the rest of the paper. Maybe you were just too obsessed with what the popular girls were doing to pay any attention to the rest of the school."

"You're probably right." We're at the locker room now, but I'm not ready to stop talking to Peter.

"I'll wait while you change," he says. "Go ahead."

Now I'm really blushing as I make my way into the locker room and get dressed in autumn-appropriate clothes again. When I head back outside, true to his word, Peter is crouched down in the hallway waiting for me. He stands up, and we walk back out toward the Carnival on the sports field.

We open the door to go back outside, and I stop short when I see how crowded the sports field is. There are way more than five hundred people there, and it looks like everyone is having a great time. There's no question — "Juicy Gossip" definitely got people to show up at the Fall Carnival. They presold more tickets than ever before, and I think a lot of people bought tickets at the door, too.

Mrs. Liu is in the dunk tank, there's a haunted maze, tons of games, and a huge food area. The school board has also set up a small booth in one corner of the field, handing out info about the referendum they're working on to help secure more money for school programs. They're going to be crowning the King and Queen at the end of the Carnival this year, rather than the beginning, to help make sure people stick around all night to play games and buy food.

Peter and I survey the crowd for a few minutes before I hear my name being called from near the food booths. Keisha is waving madly, holding an ice-cream cone.

"Jenna!" she calls. "You need to see this!"

I jog over, eager to find out what's going on. Keisha leads me through the crowd, with Peter close behind. We walk past a ton of food tables, all of which are packed with customers. Peter waves to his parents at the Moo La La booth. They stop scooping ice cream only long enough for a quick wave.

The food booths at Fall Carnival are the thing I'm most proud of. Stacey and I talked to all the food court vendors last week, and suggested they set up concessions booths at our Carnival. They were all really excited, and agreed to donate their profits to Washington Middle School in exchange for the great advertising they were getting by being a part of the Carnival. Mrs. J agreed to let us give each of the food booths a free ad in an upcoming issue of the *Washington News*, too. It's a win-win situation for everyone.

Mrs. Liu has also set up a contest. The booth that sells the most food tonight can sell their product at all our sports games. Doing the concessions at our games means a ton of business, and I know my dad is really hoping Juice It wins. Judging from the line at our smoothie stand all night, it looks like they have a good shot.

Keisha is pulling my hand, leading me toward one corner of the food area. I look up just in time to see my dad juggling three mini pineapples, all while balancing a plum on his nose. He looks like a clown.

There are probably a hundred people gathered around the Juice It stand, watching and cheering as my dad hams it up. I cover my face, embarrassed, thinking it can't get any worse. But of course, it can.

My dad sees me in the crowd and shouts for me to come over. He puts a plush pineapple hat atop my head, and hands me an apron. He wants me to work at my own school carnival? My dad does a final spin and toss of his fruit, then bows to the crowd, recommending they all try the special Little Miss Mango drink. Apparently this is something he created just for tonight. I look at Liz, and she just shrugs, grinning from ear to ear.

Finally, the crowd around the Juice It booth breaks up, and I'm left standing next to my dad and Liz, absentmindedly slicing a watermelon. Junior is wearing a grass skirt and dancing the hula in the middle of the field. He's no help at all.

Keisha and Peter walk over to chat with Chris Dotman, who bought an ice-cream cone from the

Moo La La booth. They're all really into basket-ball, and are arguing about college teams. I make a mental note to try to recruit Peter to write some sports articles for the paper.

"We need you here in the booth for just a few minutes, Jenna," my dad says.

I look at him like he's crazy. "Okay, Dad," I say reluctantly. "If you really need me to help, I'm all yours."

"It's just . . ." My dad starts to say something, then breaks off, looking at Liz.

She pulls a little box out from under her apron and hands it to me. "You earned this, Jenna."

I open the box. My very own little cell phone is nestled inside, in a tiny cluster of plastic grass. I turn it on and see that it's already been activated. There's an image of a mango as my wallpaper. "Cute, huh?" my dad says, clearly proud of his joke. "It's a little mango!"

I laugh. "I get it. Thanks so much for the phone. This is great!"

"You've been a big help in getting Juice It up and running," he says, acting all serious and fatherly. "We really appreciate it." He looks sort of misty-eyed, which doesn't really sur-prise me.

Liz pulls a hands-free cord out of her apron pocket and says, "I want you to wear this. I'm still worried about brain tumors, so promise me you'll keep the phone far away from your ears."

"You got it, Liz." I smile reassuringly. But all I can think is, *I have a phone! My very own phone!*

"And Jenna," my dad continues, "Mrs. Liu and a girl named Stacey Smith came by earlier tonight looking for you. Mrs. Liu said this year's Fall Carnival is the most successful in Washington's history. They've raised enough money that the school's activities should be safe for next year."

Keisha and Peter return to the booth just in time to hear my dad. Keisha whoops and holds up her hand for a high five. "Nice, Jenna!"

"I think we have things under control here, Jenna," my dad says, grinning as he grabs five kiwis from a bowl. "Juice It Juggling, Act Two, is about to begin. You may want to get out of here — I've never done five before!"

I pull off my pineapple hat and apron. Peter, Keisha, and I walk into the games part of the Carnival, far from my dad's juggling nightmare. Keisha stops to play a quick game of ring toss. As Peter and I stand watching, I pull my phone out of my pocket and flip it open again.

"New phone?" Peter asks.

"Yup," I say proudly. "My payment for working at Juice It. This makes it totally worth it."

Peter reaches into his pocket and pulls out his own phone. "Can I get your number?"

"Oh," I stammer. "Sure." The flush returns to my cheeks. Peter wants my number!

I flip through the options on my phone, and eventually find my own number. As soon as I finish reading it to Peter, I see a little envelope icon pop up on screen. My very first text. I hit OPEN:

Got your number from your dad. Looks like Little Miss Mango should write about herself next week . . . say hi to Peter, you flirt!

I look around, desperate to know who has my new cell number and who's watching me. From across the field, I see Stacey Smith looking my way. She's all dolled up in her Princess dress, preparing to crown the Fall Carnival Queen. She waves when she sees me looking at her, then smiles and turns away. Peter walks over to watch Keisha at the ring toss, so I hit REPLY, and type:

Little Miss Mango is out of print. Thanks for everything, Stacey. :)

Then I snap my phone closed and rejoin my friends. "Jenna, you're back!" Keisha declares as I walk up behind her and Peter, who are both admiring the stuffed pig Keisha just won.

I link arms with my best friend. Little Miss Mango is gone for good — and the real Jenna is back!

check out

ACCIDENTALLY

Friends

BY LiSA PAPADEMETRIOU

Another

candy apple book . . .

Just for you.

candy
APPLE

Amy's Wedding Rule: Everyone has parents. Try not to freak out if they start dancing.

"Do you think anyone would notice if I just ducked under the table?" My good friend, Jenelle Renwick, toyed with the edge of the white linen tablecloth. "I could just hang out here until the band stops playing."

I grinned. "Can't deal with your mom doing the Funky Waggle?" The Waggle was a dance craze that must have swept the country about thirty years ago, because all of our parents seemed to know it. My mom and dad were on the dance floor, too.

"I'm not sure who's worse," Jenelle admitted. "Mom or Great-Uncle Norman."

Jenelle glanced to one end of the dance floor, where a heavyset man with a red face was shaking his hips and letting out excited whoops in time to the beat. Jenelle's mom, Linda, was at the center of the floor in her elegant ivory wedding gown. She and my uncle Steve were laughing and dancing. Actually, Linda and Steve were decent dancers. I didn't think Jenelle had too much to be embarrassed about.

"They look like they're having the time of their lives," I said, half to myself.

"Amy Flowers, are you serious?" Jenelle demanded, sliding her fork through the moist slice of white cake on the delicate china plate in front of her. "They look like mental patients!" She was smiling when she said it, and I could tell that she thought her mom and Steve were cute.

I sneaked a glance over toward the large table by the back of the room, where a large punch bowl was set up. Beside it was a huge display of chocolate cupcakes topped with elaborate frosted sunflowers. This was the groom's cake, and at the end of the night everyone would receive a box with a cupcake in it as a party favor. If the cupcakes were half as good as the cake, they would probably be the best party favors in the history of the known universe.

"More iced tea?" asked a voice.

"Definitely!" It was some "peach-mango infusion" thing and just about the best drink I'd ever had. I held out my glass and the busboy winked a chocolatey brown eye at me. My mouth fell open. "Scott?" I nearly dropped my glass in surprise.

"Whoa — steady," he said. "Don't want this to end up all over your dress."

"What-what are you doing here?" I asked as I tried to get a grip — in more ways than one. It was taking a long time for me to process what was going on. Scott Lawton, my crush from Allington Academy, was here. He was a busboy at my friend's mom's wedding. He was serving me peach-mango iced tea. For a brief moment, I wondered if I was on hidden camera or something.

Scott shrugged. "My dad has some pretty strict ideas about allowances and stuff. As in — he won't give me one. He's had a job since he was eleven, so he thinks everyone else should, too. My mom hooked me up with this catering job. A friend of hers owns the company."

"Can't your dad give you a job at his company?" I asked. Scott's father owns a super-cool video game company.

Scott grinned, revealing his perfect teeth. I couldn't help noticing how cute he was in his long white apron. "Dad says he'll give me an internship when I'm a senior in high school, but only if I prove myself," Scott said. "And it'll be unpaid, anyway, so I'll still have to work somewhere else if I want spending money."

"Your dad is seriously tough." Jenelle looked impressed.

I was kind of impressed, too. The school we went to was one of the most exclusive private academies in Texas, and many of the Allington parents acted like glorified cash machines. Not my parents, though. I was on a scholarship. We weren't poor, but I didn't roll up to school in a chauffeur-driven limo, either, like half of my classmates.

"He's strict about some things," Scott admitted. "So, hey, are you guys excited about Crazy Week?"

"I can't wait," I gushed. Crazy Week is an Allington Academy tradition. The last week before summer vacation, the school hosts all kinds of fun activities — like Field Day, for example, and Senior Sing. We still have to go to some classes and stuff, but we finished our final exams last Friday. Nobody really takes the lessons during Crazy Week seriously — not even the teachers.

Scott glanced over toward the kitchen, where a slim man in a gray suit was frowning in our direction. "I see my manager over there giving me the evil eye. Better move on to the next table. See you around."

"See you," I called as Scott walked calmly toward the next table, holding out the silver pitcher of iced tea.

"And speaking of the evil eye," Jenelle added as she looked past Scott. Fiona Von Steig was seated three tables away, stabbing the piece of cake in front of her with her fork. She looked like a deranged cake murderer.

My heart sank at little at the sight of Fiona. "Why is she here?"

"I guess her parents made her come," Jenelle said. "They were all invited months ago — before . . . everything . . ." Jenelle's voice trailed off. She and Fiona used to be best friends. Then they had a fight. Fiona and I used to be friends, too. Well, almost. We were getting there. But then we had a fight, too.

That's kind of the way things go with Fiona.

I sighed. "I still feel bad," I admitted.

"Because you blamed Fiona for something Lucia did?" Jenelle asked. "It was an honest mistake. Fiona had tricked you lots of times before."

"Still, I shouldn't have said all of those things about how she didn't even know what real friends were." I winced at the memory. I'd been pretty harsh.

"Well . . ." Jenelle toyed with the rim of her water glass. "I guess you could always apologize. If you wanted."

"I've tried."

Jenelle shrugged. "You could try again." She gave me a knowing look, and I sighed again. I knew what she was saying — a few weeks had passed. Maybe Fiona was over it.

I hesitated. "Are *you* going to apologize?"

"That's different — Fiona really *did* trick me," Jenelle shot back. Her hand trembled a bit, and I could tell she was still angry about the way that Fiona had tried to get Jenelle to break up with her crush, Anderson. "She's the one who should apologize."

Just then, Fiona stood up and moved toward the punch table. My heart started pounding then, the way it does when I'm about to do something scary. It's like my body knows what I'm going to do before my brain does. In a flash, I found myself on my feet. I started after her before I had a chance to really think about it.

"What are you doing?" Jenelle whispered.

"I'm going to try one more time," I told her. I didn't know how Fiona would react. But if I apologized, at least I wouldn't have to feel like I was having a heart attack every time I saw her.

"Fiona," I said, and she turned to face me.

Her blue eyes narrowed when she saw me. "Oh, look who it is." Her voice was colder than the ice cubes floating in the punch. "Amy Flowers. Are you going to accuse me of stealing a cupcake?" She gestured toward the groom's cake display.

I suddenly regretted coming over. But I wasn't going to give up that easily. "No, I-I just wanted to say that I'm sorry. I'm sorry that I mistrusted you. And I'm sorry . . . for what I said."

Fiona's face softened. "Really?" she asked.

"Really," I said warmly. "I mean, we were really becoming friends." I thought about how I'd spent the night at her house, and the quiet time we'd shared in her kitchen as the sun came up. Fiona could be difficult. But she could be sweet, too.

"Wow, Amy, that means so much to me." Fiona blinked a little, as if she was fighting tears, although I didn't see any. She reached out and pressed my hand. "Thank you."

"Y-you're welcome," I stammered. *Wow.* I don't know what I'd been expecting . . . but this sure was a shock. My head felt light. *I did the right thing,* I thought. *Fiona forgives me.* Maybe we wouldn't be friends. But we didn't have to be enemies, either. "Well, I-I guess I'm going to head back to my table."

"I'm *so* glad we talked," Fiona said.

"Me, too." I smiled at her. Impulsively, I reached out and gave her a quick hug.

Fiona patted my back awkwardly. "Oh, and Amy?" She smiled at me.

"Yes?"

"Have a cupcake," she said. In one lightning move, she plucked one of the small supports holding up the bottom tier of the display. She jumped back as three hundred chocolate cupcakes toppled — all over me. The silver platters clanged and clattered to the floor, and bits of cake and gobs of icing flew everywhere. The band stopped playing and everyone turned to look. Fiona had somehow managed to disappear.

CANDY APPLE BOOKS

Drama Queen

I've Got a Secret

Confessions of a
Bitter Secret Santa

The Boy Next Door

The Sister Switch

The Accidental
Cheerleader

The Babysitting Wars

Star-Crossed

Read them all!

Accidentally
Fabulous

Accidentally
Famous

Accidentally
Fooled

Accidentally
Friends

How to Be a Girly Girl
in Just Ten Days

Miss Popularity

Miss Popularity
Goes Camping

Making Waves

Life, Starring Me!

Juicy Gossip

Callie for President

Totally Crushed

AkE YOU READY FOR MIDDLE SCHOOL?

After studying her Middle School handbook, Jenny is totally ready for sixth grade—she and her BFF, Addie, are sure to have a blast!

But when Jenny meets Addie at their lockers the next day, it looks like Addie has other plans—that don't include her. Is Addie ditching Jenny for the Pops—the coolest seventh graders in the school?

HOW I SURVIVED MIDDLE SCHOOL

Can You Get an F in Lunch?

MSCHOLASTIC

BY NANCY KRULIK

HOW I SURVIVED MIDDLE SCHOOL

Madame President

BY NANCY KRULIK

HOW I SURVIVED MIDDLE SCHOOL

I Heard a Rumor

BY NANCY KRULIK

HOW I SURVIVED MIDDLE SCHOOL

The New Girl

NANCY KRULIK